The *Past* COMES HOME

SILVIA VIOLET

Silvia Violet

The Past Comes Home by Silvia Violet

Chapter One

1997

Pax slouched on the ragged couch in his basement rec room, pretending to read a comic. He was actually listening to his brother, Rob, and Rob's best friend, Brad. Brad was tall, with broad shoulders and a smile that had girls ready to do anything for a chance to go out with him. Not that Pax noticed such things. It wasn't like *he* was a girl or anything. But Brad was captain of the football team, swim-team star, and a straight-A student. Who didn't notice him? When Brad came over, Pax could barely resist following him and Rob around. He was drawn to Brad in a way he didn't understand. Hero worship, that was it. Most guys at Ames Bridge High envied or admired Brad. Why shouldn't Pax?

In the complex social order at their high school, Rob fell below the upper echelon of sports stars and cheerleaders, but nowhere near as far down as Pax. While the star of the senior class might not typically hang around with a regular guy like Rob, his brother and Brad had been friends since Brad's family moved to this little town in central North Carolina when they were in second grade. On the first day of school, their teacher asked Rob to help Brad find his way around, and after all these years, they still hung out every weekend.

"Look what Julie gave me." Pax glanced up to see his brother hand Brad a CD.

Brad grinned. "She burned you a CD, huh? What's on it?"

Rob shrugged. "I don't know. She pushed it into my hand as I was running to play practice."

Brad looked down at the CD cover. "*Rob's Mix*. She even wrote it in bubble letters with a little pink heart above the *i*. How precious."

Rob flipped Brad off, and Brad chuckled.

The deep, resonating sound made Pax's heart speed up. From embarrassment, right? Yeah, that explained his reaction. He was embarrassed to listen in on a conversation about his brother and some girl.

From what Pax could see, it looked like Julie had made a list of the song titles and slipped it in the cover. Brad seemed to be reading through them. "Ooh. Madonna's 'Open Your Heart.' She must really like you."

Rob groaned. "Yeah. She was with Danielle when she gave it to me, and their faces were so fucking red, I thought they were going to explode."

Brad laughed again. "I can just hear them." He did a high-pitched imitation of Julie's giggle.

Pax failed to hold in a snicker.

"Shut up, Pax!" Rob delivered a kick to his leg. "What are you doing in here, anyway?"

"Leave him alone," Brad said. "Anytime now, the kid will be getting CDs of his own from girls. I can see it now—*Pax's Mix*, all decorated with hearts and flowers."

"Gross!" Pax didn't want stupid flowery music mixes, but Brad's defense of him made his stomach feel strange. He was hot and cold at the same time. *Am I getting sick?*

"Are you gonna ask her out?" Brad directed the comment at Rob.

"I don't know. She's only a sophomore, but she *is* kinda hot."

"Is she?" Brad didn't look convinced.

"You don't think so? I mean, those tits." He cupped his hands in front of his chest to indicate Julie's assets.

Brad shrugged. "I haven't really noticed."

Rob rolled his eyes. "For someone so smart, you can be a real space cadet."

Brad ignored him as he opened the CD case and took out the disc.

"What are you doing?" Rob asked.

"I want to hear it."

"Why?" Rob wrinkled his nose in disgust.

"'Open Your Heart' is like my favorite song."

Pax liked how Brad wasn't what he seemed, but he didn't quite understand why thinking about that made him feel so twisted up inside.

"You're kidding me, right? Do your football buddies know that?"

Brad scowled in mock anger. "Don't knock the Queen of Pop."

Rob laughed. "Sometimes I just don't get you."

Brad stuck the CD into the old player Pax's family had relegated to the basement. He hit skip a few times, and then "Open Your Heart" blared out from the speakers.

Brad sang right along with it. After a minute

or two, Pax gave up pretending to read and turned so he could see Brad. As the song faded, Backstreet's "Quit Playing Games (With My Heart)" came on. Pax wondered how Brad would look wet, with his shirt clinging to him like the band in the video. In that moment he realized what he was feeling for Brad was definitely not hero worship. Unlike his brother, he wasn't ever going to go after a girl for her big tits. He wasn't going to go after a girl at all.

Chapter Two

2015

Rain pounded the sidewalk as Brad hurried to his car. In the time it took him to fold his umbrella so he could close the car door, he was soaked. At least the weather matched his mood. Thirty-six was way too young to die, and yet it had happened to Rob. Instantly. A stretch of dark road, a driver losing control of a semi, and he was gone. Brad didn't get to say goodbye. In fact, he hadn't said a damn thing to Rob in almost three years, not since… But there was no point in dwelling on it. Brad couldn't change the past, but that didn't mean it hurt any less. Even before he fucked up his relationship with Rob, they hadn't kept up with each other the way he'd thought they would. Rob had returned to Ames Bridge after college, and Brad had moved to Chicago. After he'd lived there a while, he began to see the world very differently than people back home.

But that didn't mean he didn't miss his friend.

He sat in the driver's seat, trying to hold back tears. No point in being one of the first ones to leave the funeral home. It would be a while before Rob's family made it back to their house. The private graveside service would take longer than usual to get through in this weather, and he was sure they'd be driving slowly, the bad road conditions making a horrible day even worse.

Should he even go to the house? Did Rob's family know he and Rob had fought? Had Rob told them what he'd said? They'd certainly treated him civilly at the visitation the night before, Pax especially so. He'd seemed relieved to see Brad. And Brad had sure as hell enjoyed seeing him. Pax had taken a job in Savannah after graduating from Savannah College of Art and Design. Their visits back to Ames Bridge had rarely coincided, and the few times they had seen each other in recent years, it was only in passing as he headed out with Rob.

But now…

No platitudes were going to make this any better. Maybe he should just go back to his hotel and drink himself to sleep.

No. He remembered the look on Pax's face when he'd walked into the visitation. He'd looked at Brad like he was a lifeline, someone who could help Pax make sense of this tragedy. He'd stay for Pax. Hell, he'd do just about anything for him.

Once there was no longer a steady stream of cars exiting the church parking lot, Brad put his car in gear and backed out of his space.

He didn't want to face his sterile, empty hotel room, not without a bottle of Scotch, anyway. So he drove to Trish's diner. Like him, Trish had been at the funeral, as had many of her employees, but he doubted she'd shut the place down. When he pulled into the parking lot, he saw lights on and a sparse crowd inside.

Then he noticed Trish pulling into a space at the back of the lot. He opened his large umbrella and hurried down the sidewalk so they could share it.

When they'd gotten through the side door and dried their feet on the mat, Trish pulled him into a tight hug.

"How are you?" she asked when they stepped apart.

"I—"

She held up a hand. "Forgive me. That was a terrible question. You're torn up about Rob like the rest of us. I figured you'd be heading over to the Marshalls' house."

"I will once they've had time to get back there."

She nodded. "Would you mind taking over a few pies for me? I took the whole morning off, and I'm short-staffed, what with it being summer and several of my waitresses on vacation."

"Of course I will."

"Thanks, honey. Now have a seat at the counter. Whatever you want, it's on the house."

Brad shook his head. "No, that's not right."

"It is if I say so."

Brad sighed. He knew better than to argue with Trish; everyone in Ames Bridge did. He'd just leave a huge tip. She couldn't stop him from doing that.

He took a seat, and a few moments later Trish came out from the back with a bright-red apron tied around her ample waist and a glass of tea in her hand. She set the glass in front of him. "Tell me what else you'd like."

Brad frowned. Despite having chosen to come to the diner, he wasn't actually hungry. "I'm not sure.

I just… I haven't had much appetite since I heard about Rob."

"You two were about as close as could be when you were kids."

"Yeah. And…" Brad took a deep breath. He was not going to have a breakdown sitting at Trish's counter. "I wish we'd stayed that way."

Trish laid a hand over his. "People grow and change. They go their own ways, but that doesn't mean they love each other less."

Brad sighed. "I… Maybe, sometimes, but…"

"Not two months ago, Rob was in here with Roscoe. They were talking about high school. Roscoe mentioned something about you, and Rob started talking about how you never treated him differently just because he wasn't a jock, how you didn't care if someone was cool or athletic or anything else. You chose your friends based on whether you enjoyed talking to them. Trust me, he still cared about you."

Her words should have made Brad feel better. Instead, all he could think was why hadn't Rob called if he felt that way.

Why didn't you call him?

Brad tried to stand and nearly fell off his stool. "Trish, I… I just…"

"Come on back to the kitchen, honey."

She came around the counter and steadied him with an arm around his waist. When they got to the back, she opened the door of the tiny break room, which was thankfully empty. "Take your time. I won't let anyone else go in."

Brad tried to say thank you, but the words wouldn't come out.

The springs groaned as he sank onto the ancient couch. Even there in private, he tried to fight his grief, but after a few seconds tears began to roll down his cheeks. He pressed his hand to his mouth to keep from making any noise, but otherwise he let go, letting the flood of emotion that had been threatening to overtake him rush out.

He wasn't sure how long he sat there, sobbing over his lost time with Rob, the way Rob had hurt him, the fact that he'd waited so long to share his secret.

Did you have to tell him you had a crush on his brother?

That was what had pushed Rob over the line. Rob had been angry that Brad had waited to tell him he was gay, that he'd assumed Rob wouldn't accept him, but he would probably have gotten over that if Brad hadn't added that he'd wanted Pax as far back as high school. He'd thought full disclosure was best. He'd been wrong.

Stay away from my brother. If you can't be honest with me, then I don't trust you with him.

Those were the last words Rob ever said to him. Brad had walked away then, too angry to respond with anything he wouldn't regret. Now, he regretted his silence more.

***

While balancing the boxes of pie Trish had given him, Brad held the door of the Marshalls' house for an elderly couple who were leaving as he arrived. After his breakdown at the diner, he'd decided he needed a shower and a drink before he could face Pax or his parents. Trish had sent him away with a club sandwich, and he'd managed to eat almost half of it while he was at his hotel.

Once the couple had passed, he stepped into the house crowded with guests. The paint colors had changed, and he spotted a few unfamiliar pieces of furniture. Otherwise, except for the picture on the wall that showed Rob and Pax as adults rather than children, the house was unchanged. How many hours had he spent here growing up? Nearly as many as he spent at his own house if he didn't count sleeping. Of course he'd slept over at Rob's plenty of times too. They'd spread out their sleeping bags in the basement rec room, and Rob's mom had always made popcorn when they'd watched movies. He remembered watching the original *Star Wars* trilogy countless times when they were kids. Back then their only option had been VHS cassettes. Oh, how they'd hated waiting for them to rewind.

Maybe in honor of those old times, he'd rent *Return of the Jedi* that night. It was his personal favorite, and that had absolutely nothing to do with how incredibly sexy Han was in it.

Suddenly, Brad realized he was standing in the middle of the foyer as people flowed around him.

Just go in the kitchen, pay your respects, and you can leave.

Still, he didn't move. It had been so awkward talking to Rob's parents the night before. He wasn't sure he could do it again.

You're an adult. You run your own business. You know how to handle basic social situations.

A funeral for an acquaintance or a colleague, yes, but not this. There was no etiquette lesson to prepare you for what to say when your best friend from childhood, who'd cut off all contact with you, died suddenly.

"Brad?" He turned and saw Pax. He had hardly changed in the five or six years since their visits to Ames Bridge had last coincided. He had the same dark, wavy hair, the same dark eyes that Brad had trouble looking away from. The glasses were different, but they suited him, cool without overstating it. But the look of anguish in his eyes was what made Brad's heart skip a beat. Brad would do anything to take that horror away from him.

"Um…hi."

Pax's gaze dropped to the boxes he was holding. "You brought food?"

Heat filled Brad's face. He should have brought something himself instead of just what Trish gave him. But what else could he bring? He'd sent flowers to the church. "They're pies. From Trish. She asked me to bring them over."

Pax tilted his head as if considering something. "I might actually be able to eat pie."

"You haven't had any appetite either?"

Pax shook his head. "Not much. My mom forced an egg on me this morning, but I'm just all…"

His words trailed off, and they stood there looking at each other.

"Um…should I take these to the kitchen?" Brad asked a few seconds later.

"What kind are they?"

"I'm not sure. One of them is cherry. I think the others might be apple and pecan."

"Wait here," Pax said. "I mean if you

don't—"

"Whatever you need. I'll do it."

"Okay. I'll be right back."

Pax took the boxes from him and headed toward the kitchen. Brad stepped to the side so he wasn't blocking people from getting through, and waited for Pax to return. When he did, he was still carrying one of the boxes. "I need some air. Will you come with me?"

"Sure." Brad didn't ask about the box; he just followed Pax outside.

They walked through the side gate into the backyard. Brad shut the gate behind them, and Pax blew out a long breath. "I was suffocating in there. I can't talk to anyone else. I just…"

Pax was pale, and he looked ready to collapse. Brad reached out to steady him. The second his hand closed around Pax's arm, he felt a jolt of current zing through him. Pax looked up, his eyes wide.

Shit, he'd felt it too. His lips parted like he was going to say something, but he didn't. Brad could feel the heat of Pax's body through the fabric of his shirt and jacket. What would it feel like if he touched bare skin?

No, this was not the time to think of that.

He turned away and tugged on Pax's arm.

"Let's go."

"Where?"

"The tree house."

Pax looked down at his dark suit. "I don't think—"

"I do. It's the only place around here where we'll have complete privacy." Unless… No, taking

Pax back to his hotel was a terrible idea. If he were alone with Pax in a room dominated by an enormous bed, with all these crazy emotions racing through him, he would kiss him like he wanted to do right now. And if Pax felt what Brad did, kissing would lead to them making use of the enormous bed, and then Brad would hate himself for seducing Pax after his brother's funeral. Rob had no right to tell Brad not to pursue Pax, but only a vile person would defy the wishes of a dead man on the day he was put to rest.

Brad took the box from Pax and started up the ladder to the tree house, praying his hands were steady enough not to drop the pie. He glanced back and saw that Pax was still on the ground. "Come on."

"I shouldn't."

"You need a break. It's okay to take a few minutes away."

"But my mom and dad…"

"Is someone with them?"

"Yeah, Irene and Elsie and their church circle are basically running things in there."

Brad smiled. Of course they were. "That means your parents are in good hands. And you have your phone, right?"

Pax nodded.

"Then come on."

Pax looked over his shoulder once more, probably checking to see if anyone was looking. Then he put his foot on the first rung of the ladder. Satisfied that he'd follow, Brad resumed climbing. He set the pie on the floor of the tree house and hoisted himself up through the hole.

When he glanced around he saw that the place

was empty now except for some leaves and pollen. The carpet squares, pillows, and varying stacks of supplies for whatever game he and Rob—and later Pax and his friends—were playing were no longer there.

Pax emerged and settled on the floor beside him, frowning at the dust that was getting on his suit.

"It will brush off, don't worry."

"Yeah, I guess so," Pax said as he opened the box.

"It's the cherry one," Pax added, even though that was obvious. "I know Trish meant for it to be shared, but—"

"Trish meant to let you know she cared. If eating the pie all by yourself is what you need, then that's what she'd want you to do."

"I don't want to eat it by myself," Pax said.

"You don't?"

"No, I want to eat it with you."

He looked at Brad, and Brad's heart skipped a beat. Pax used to look at him like that when he was a teenager, like he thought Brad was everything. He wasn't, not then and not now. But he'd like to be more to Pax than he'd been back then.

Stay away from my brother. Rob's words echoed in his mind.

Not today, but maybe sometime in the future. Brad bit back a sigh. Who was he kidding? He lived a thousand miles away, and he wasn't sure he'd ever stop hearing those words from Rob.

Pax pulled two plastic forks from his jacket pocket and handed one to Brad. "I know this is hard for you."

Brad shook his head. "He was your brother." He laid a hand over Pax's, and that zing happened again. *Don't make eye contact.*

"But you were so close to him and…"

"It sucks for both of us, but you need comfort now, and I want to give it to you." Oh God, did he.

Pax stabbed his fork into the pie and brought a bite to his mouth. After chewing, he said, "This is the first thing I've tasted that doesn't make me feel sick."

The smell of the pie overpowered Brad. He'd thought he wasn't hungry, but now he needed a taste.

He reached out his fork tentatively.

"Go ahead. I'm really not going to eat the whole thing."

They didn't say much else, but the silence was companionable rather than awkward. Between the two of them, they very nearly finished the pie off. Then they lay back on the hard wooden floor of the tree house with their hands over their stomachs.

"Ugh. I should've stopped a lot earlier," Pax said.

"You and me both."

He laughed. "Thank you."

"Thank *you* for sharing your pie. I needed that."

"I needed you."

Oh shit.

He doesn't mean it like that, you idiot.

"I mean…"

Brad gave a nervous laugh. "It's okay. I understand. You needed someone you could be yourself around."

"Yeah, I knew you wouldn't care if I just

wanted to hide and stuff my face with pie."

"I'll always be here for you when you need to eat half a pie."

Brad expected him to laugh, but instead Pax turned and looked at him. He had to squeeze his hands into fists to keep from reaching out to touch Pax's face. He wanted to kiss him so badly. Why did Pax have to be the one man who'd ever had such a strong effect on him? It wasn't that Brad hadn't wanted other men. He'd dated—and hooked up— plenty, but no one else made electricity rush through him just from touching a suit-clad arm.

He forced himself to sit up. "I should probably go in and speak to your parents."

"Yeah, they'll want to see you."

"After that I'll need to head back to my hotel. I have an early flight."

"Oh, you're leaving tomorrow." Pax looked so disappointed that for a few seconds, Brad contemplated changing his flight. But Pax had friends and family here, and Brad wasn't sure he could spend more time around him and not betray his promise to Rob's memory.

"I am. I've got…work."

Pax placed the forks in the box and closed the lid. When they reached the bottom of the ladder, he turned to face Brad. He was so close. If they were alone… If Rob were still alive… If Brad didn't live so far away…

Brad stepped past him. "I'll go in first so you can slip back out again if it's too bad."

Pax nodded, but he didn't say anything.

Brad spent a few minutes talking with Mr. and

Mrs. Marshall, and then more than a few minutes with Irene, whose son Scott had been a close friend of his. Brad wondered just how long she could talk without taking a breath. She could probably set a record. When he finally managed to sneak away, he didn't see Pax anywhere.

Go look for him.

No, that will just make things worse.

This isn't about you. It's about him.

But Brad was grieving too—Rob's death as well as what might have been with Pax. If things were different... But they weren't. He slipped out of the kitchen, then walked through the foyer and out the front door.

Chapter Three

2017

Pax lay on his bed, staring at the ceiling. Today he'd be seeing Brad for the first time since Rob's funeral. Brad, the man he'd had a crush on for twenty fucking years. How pathetic was that? He'd thought Brad would've changed more in all those years, that the man he imagined Brad to be was nothing but a fantasy. He'd been wrong. Brad was everything he remembered, but all grown up and even hotter. He'd wanted him so badly the day of the funeral. He'd wanted to grab him, kiss him, and offer his ass right there in the tree house, after they'd just put his brother in the ground. Nothing like throwing yourself at a straight man at your brother's funeral.

Pax had tried not to think about Brad in the weeks that followed. He'd tried not to think about Rob either. He'd failed on both counts. And then months later, after his mother had a stroke that he believed was caused by grief more than anything else, he'd moved back to Ames Bridge. Neither of his parents had been handling their loss well, and they needed him.

Now Brad was coming to town for his twentieth high school reunion, and Pax was going to see him again. Pax hadn't had any desire to go to his own reunions, and he sure as hell wouldn't travel as far as Brad was—all the way from Chicago—for one. But if you were the captain of the football team, Pax supposed you felt some sort of obligation to show up for the big ones.

When he'd gotten a text from Brad saying he'd be in town and would love to get together, his stomach had done flip-flops. It was like he was fourteen all over again. And now he was going to be a zombie with bags under his eyes when Brad arrived. He'd tossed and turned for ages before finally falling asleep only to wake up a few hours later at three. It was now five, and he was once again wide awake.

He picked up his phone from the nightstand and turned on a guided meditation. Maybe that would help. He focused on his breathing. His mind started to wander, but he pulled it back to listening to the drowsy voice telling him to feel the rise and fall of his abdomen. A few seconds later, he became aware that he was reliving the day in his parents' basement when he'd first realized he liked Brad the way people expected him to like girls.

He growled in frustration, turned the meditation off, and gave in to the memories.

When he'd had that revelation at fourteen, it hadn't stopped him from trying to prove himself wrong. He didn't want to disappoint his family, lose friends, or get the shit beat out of him at school. Being a geek who preferred reading sci-fi and drawing comics to normal high school socialization was bad enough. Being a gay geek could be detrimental to his health.

So he ignored what he knew about himself and pretended he was straight for several more years.

He compartmentalized the fact that he fantasized about Brad every time he jerked off. As far as he was concerned, those were the actions of someone else, someone who took over his brain when he was alone in the dark. He pretended he didn't stare at the shirtless men in the action movies he saw with his friends. Instead, he commented on exploding cars, fast motorcycles, and big guns, though he supposed they were simply a metaphor for what he found more appealing. Pax talked about girls with his friends and gawked when it was appropriate. He even slept with a few women senior year, but he was just playacting.

When he went away to college, he started to let the mask slip. In his second year, he kissed a boy for the first time—and pretended that boy was Brad. When he turned twenty-one he told Rob and his parents he was gay. His parents acted like they'd always known, and while they were sorry he would face prejudice from a lot of others in town, their love was truly unconditional.

Rob had fallen in with a more conservative crowd in college. He wasn't thrilled by Pax's announcement, but he accepted it, and he never treated Pax any differently. Somehow, though, he didn't think Rob could handle learning that he'd had a crush on Brad since high school.

By the time Pax was working on his MFA at the Savannah College of Art and Design, he'd finally stopped comparing every man he met to Brad, though he hadn't stopped wanting him. Any time he heard "Open Your Heart," he thought about Brad nonstop for days. Rob would periodically mention how Brad was doing, but Pax never asked about him, afraid his wistful tone would give him away. Then Rob had a falling-out with Brad. He refused to tell Pax what happened, clamming up every time Pax tried to push him to work things out.

Pax had desperately wanted to call Brad in the grief-laden weeks after Rob's funeral, but for what? He doubted Brad was any more ready to reminisce about Rob than Pax was, and there really wasn't any other reason to call. Then later, when the grief wasn't so fresh, he couldn't figure out what to say, so he said nothing. Until now. Now he would have to find something to say that didn't make him sound like a lunatic or stalker.

***

Pax must have fallen asleep at some point, because he woke to the sound of his alarm blaring. It got progressively louder if it wasn't turned off, so he must have slept through it for a while because it was going full blast. He poked at it, desperate to shut it off before someone in one of the other apartments came knocking on his door to complain. He rented an apartment over the art gallery and paint-your-own-pottery shop he'd run for the last two years. The second and third floors of the building were divided into apartments, office space, and now a few art studios. Pax's place was small, but he didn't need much, and he couldn't beat the convenience of living right upstairs from where he worked.

A number of the town's residents had scoffed at the idea of an art gallery staying in business, but the city council had funneled a lot of money into revitalizing the downtown, and it was starting to pay off. The number of tourists in town had soared thanks to other local entrepreneurs like Cal McMurtry, who ran a progressive farm that was now part of the Central Carolina Farm Tour, as well as the historical society, which was now organizing demonstrations of early twentieth-century life near the covered bridge that gave the town its name.

Pax stretched and slowly made his way to the bathroom. After a shower, he still felt only marginally awake. He needed coffee desperately. He popped a capsule into his Keurig, filled the water reservoir, and turned it on. Then he opened his fridge and stared into its depths. *Damn.* He was out of the precooked turkey sausages he liked, and after so little sleep, he couldn't summon the energy to make an egg. He closed the fridge and pulled a box of brown sugar cinnamon Pop-Tarts from the cabinet. So much for protein; he was going for the sugar rush.

After he'd eaten, Pax carried his coffee downstairs and unlocked the door to the gallery. He checked the displays of his own work and those of other local artists, making sure everything was dusted and arranged to best advantage. Then he walked through the open doorway into the pottery-painting space. He had a group of first-graders coming in that morning. He loved helping the young children choose the paint colors they wanted to use on their pieces. They had none of the inhibitions of older artists when it came to planning—or not planning—a design. But no matter how fun they were, a whole class of six-year-olds would create a lot of chaos. He wasn't sure how he was going to deal with that on a few hours' sleep and with butterflies doing aerial gymnastics in his stomach in anticipation of Brad's arrival later that morning.

He drank the rest of his coffee and put the mug down on the desk in the gallery office. He needed another cup or six, though he doubted anything would truly wake him up.

Maybe some music would help. He scrolled through the playlist on the old phone he used as an iPod. Even after listening to it the night before, he still had "Open Your Heart" stuck in his mind, so he gave in to the temptation of his vintage Madonna playlist, which of course started with the song he still connected with his sexual awakening. He hit Play and let it take him back to ninth grade. Sure, he was torturing himself by reliving those teenage fantasies, but if he was going to see Brad, he might as well play the appropriate soundtrack.

The song poured from the speakers, and within seconds, Pax was dancing around the store, singing as he cleaned tables and reorganized the supplies. He would've done those things the night before if he hadn't been too exhausted after the monthly Paint with Wine evening, in which a lot of the respectable women of Ames Bridge drank an obscene amount of wine and spilled the most scandalous gossip. He was anxious about Brad coming to town, but at least he wasn't hungover like many of the attendees likely were.

A knock on the shop door drew his attention; probably his assistant, Cindy. It wouldn't be the first time she'd forgotten her key, and no one else would be dropping by this early. Microfiber duster in hand, he twirled his way past the worktables and the unpainted pottery pieces customers chose from.

The Past Comes Home

He sang along with Madonna as he reached for the doorknob, and froze—Brad was grinning at him through the front window.

Chapter Four

Heat rushed to Pax's face. For a moment he contemplated racing over to turn the music off, then walking calmly back to the door as if the last few seconds had never happened. Could he convince Brad his earlier appearance was a hallucination?

Brad placed his hand against the window and peered in. "Is this a bad time? I know I'm really early."

"Um…no. Just a sec."

He would open the damn door, talk to Brad, and generally behave like a respectable adult. That's what would happen.

With a deep breath, he turned the knob and stared, openmouthed, unable to form a single word. Was Brad even more gorgeous than he'd been two years ago? At eighteen he'd been the hottest boy in school, but now with his dirty-blond hair showing hints of gray, he was even better. His T-shirt stretched taut over his biceps, and his jeans fit like they were tailor-made for his muscular thighs. But the thing that made Brad even more desirable now was how relaxed and happy he seemed. In high school he'd always been restless, as though he were uncomfortable in his gorgeous body, despite having it made as far as anyone else could tell. Pax wondered what had changed.

Pax looked up at Brad and realized he'd been

caught giving him a blatant once-over while he stood in the doorway. "Um… Where are my manners?" Fled in the face of his insanity? "Come in. That is, if you'd like to."

"I would." He smiled, showing off the dimple in his left cheek.

Pax wanted to run his tongue across it. Instead, he made a dramatic show of bowing and sweeping his hand toward the interior. "Enter, sir."

Brad laughed and stepped inside. Pax shut the door behind him and locked it, hoping Cindy would be late so he'd have time to show Brad the gallery without anyone else there.

"Is it '80s day?" Brad asked.

Pax needed to accept that he would be blushing the whole time Brad was there. "No, I was just cleaning, and this music motivates me."

"Let me know if I'm keeping you from something. I woke up early, and I was anxious to see you."

Anxious to see him? Him? Pax's knees threatened to give. Was it possible…? No. Just because Pax had spent far too many hours fantasizing about Brad saying he was gay or bi, that didn't mean it was going to happen.

Pax set the duster down on a shelf of cleaning supplies. *Just tell him about the shop like you would anyone else.*

But before he could direct them, Brad headed toward the large, open doorway that led into the gallery. Pax followed him as he made a beeline for one of Pax's paintings that hung on the far wall, an abstract vision of a sunset filled with swirling shades of orange, red, and purple.

"This is yours, isn't it?" he asked.

His deep voice did strange things to Pax's insides. "Yes."

"It's amazing. The colors are just…wow."

"Thanks. It's one of my favorite pieces." Pax was particularly proud of it, but he had no idea how Brad had been able to identify the painting as his.

He smiled again and gave Pax a look that made him want to get on his knees and offer Brad some true thanks.

"When I looked you up online and saw the work you'd been doing, I was so impressed. You were a great artist when you were a kid, so I knew you had talent, but this is amazing. And the glasswork you do, it's stunning."

Pax had to try a few times before he could actually respond. "Y-you looked me up?"

Brad nodded as he walked over to another of Pax's abstract paintings, a mountain range in the fall. "This is yours too, right?"

Pax's heart banged against his chest so hard, he thought one of his ribs might crack. Brad had looked him up, seen his work, been anxious to see him. Why? He was just Rob's little brother. Sure, Brad had always defended him when Rob was being an ass, but he'd been nothing more than an amusing kid to Brad, hadn't he?

"Um…yeah, this is my work. Most of the other pieces you see here are made by artists who use the studio space upstairs." He gestured toward the ceiling.

"I heard the upper floors have been renovated.

My parents keep me up on the news Miss Elsie tells them."

Pax laughed. "You must be well informed, then."

"I'm sure I get the condensed version. I only have so many hours to be on the phone."

Not wanting to think too hard about what Brad knew about him, Pax said, "The second and third floors are divided into apartments, studios, and small offices. I live up there now."

"Last time I was downtown, a lot of these buildings were starting to fall apart. I'm thrilled to see so many new businesses are here now."

The revitalization was one of the things that had made moving back home bearable. "Me too. A lot more tourists are coming into town after seeing the bridge, and more people are coming from Greensboro and High Point to eat and shop. If things keep going the way they are, we could have a bona fide arts district one day."

"That's fantastic. I'm glad you stuck to doing what you wanted." Brad's bright smile was powerful enough to make him dizzy.

"What about you? I never even suspected you were interested in computers until you came home from college saying your major was computer engineering."

Brad blushed and looked away. "I kinda hid that part of me when I was in high school. Other kids would have… Well, I might not have had it so easy if everyone knew I was really a nerdy kid who stayed up half the night, tinkering with his parents' computer. They thought I was just playing games, but

I was looking at code, changing things, making it run better."

"Really?" Pax stared at him with his mouth open.

Brad laughed. "Yeah, that would have been the reaction of most of my 'friends' too, followed by them telling me to stop being such a fucking nerd and concentrate on my game so we can beat Northwest."

Pax shook his head. "Most of your friends didn't have much on their minds outside of football, did they?"

"No, except for Rob."

They were both silent for a few moments. Even after two years, it always hit Pax hard when he thought of his brother.

"So why did you hang around with those guys if you didn't have much in common?"

Brad shrugged. Pax sensed he didn't want to talk about his former friends anymore, so he steered Brad toward the front of the gallery, where various ceramics and glassware were on display. Brad pointed to ones he liked and asked some questions about how they were made. Then he stopped in front of a glass bowl with swirls of royal blue, green, and purple.

"You made this," he said, without looking at the card on the display pedestal.

"How did you know that? I just finished that piece, so it's not on the website."

He looked up, capturing Pax's gaze. "Because it looks like you."

"Really?"

He laughed. "You know what I mean. It matches the style of your painting."

"I didn't know you were into art."

Brad shuffled from one foot to the other. "I'm not really. I just…know you."

Pax gave him a look that must've shown his disbelief.

"That sounds crazy, doesn't it? Other than the day of the funeral, I haven't seen you in years, but before I came to the reunion, a couple of my friends who'd been to their own reunions warned me that no one really changes. In essence, we're all just like we were in high school. I bristled at first, thinking, 'I hope I've grown up since then,' but I think they're probably right. We're all like we were inside, like we were to those who really knew us."

Pax pondered that thought. How much had he changed? "I think you're mostly right except that…well…" Brad did know, didn't he? Surely, Rob had told him Pax was gay, or someone had. He hadn't bothered trying to hide it in ages. For God's sake, he'd been swinging his hips to Madonna while holding a duster when Brad arrived.

"What?" The intense look in Brad's eyes stole Pax's breath. He could easily get lost in their gray-green depths.

"I'd like to think I'm a better person now." He wasn't going to blurt out that he was gay. He'd been obvious enough by staring at Brad. He didn't need to make things more awkward.

Brad frowned. "You were already an amazing person in high school, one of the best I knew."

Pax's heart fluttered. "Really? Thank you."

Brad looked down at the bowl again. "I'd like to buy this."

"Why?"

Brad looked at him like he'd lost his mind. "Because it's beautiful and it reminds me of you. I've missed you."

Then why didn't you call after the funeral? "Oh."

As if Brad read Pax's mind, he said, "I meant to call after we saw each other, after Rob… I should have. But the longer I went without doing it, the harder it was to just pick up the phone. I looked you up on Facebook, but I thought it might be weird to send you a request without a message, and I didn't know what to say. Shit, I sound like an idiot."

Pax resisted the urge to lay a comforting hand on his arm. "You sound like a man who'd lost his best friend."

"But he was your brother. You needed support, and I—"

"You were amazing. That afternoon after the funeral… If you hadn't been there, I don't know how I would've gotten through it."

Brad nodded. They stood there in silence for several moments, and then Brad said, "Am I keeping you from getting work done?"

"No!" *Wow, very cool, Pax.*

Brad looked at him like he was unsure how to respond to his vehemence.

"I'm really glad you're here. But please don't feel obligated to buy anything."

Brad raised his brows. "Is that what you tell all your customers?"

"You're not a customer. You're a friend."

That won Pax a smile. "I'm glad you still

think of me that way."

Pax thought of him as far more than that. Too bad that was only a fantasy.

"I'm buying the bowl because I want to, not out of any obligation."

Did he have any idea how those words tormented Pax? "Okay, I can...um... The register is over here."

Pax picked up the bowl and carried it to the counter. He rang up the sale, and he'd just finished scanning Brad's card when a knock on the door made him jump, nearly knocking the bowl off the counter.

Brad gave him an odd look as he steadied the bowl.

"Sorry. I'm just... I've had a lot of coffee. That's probably my assistant, Cindy. She's coming in to help me set up for a school group."

Pax let Cindy in, and Brad looked around the gallery while the two of them went over what needed to be done before the kids arrived.

"I can wrap the bowl up for you," he said when he rejoined Brad.

"I'm not in a hurry if you'd rather I come back later."

Pax would rather he stay there all day, although then he wouldn't be able to concentrate on work. "Do you have plans for the afternoon? I was thinking we could...um...have lunch." *Way to articulate, Pax.*

Brad's face lit up. "I'd love that."

Oh God, what had he done? "There's a great new sandwich shop down the street. We could go there."

"Sounds good."

He had a lunch date with Brad. Okay, not a date, but he was going to get to spend more time with him, and Brad was acting very…flirtatious? No, Pax was just seeing what he wanted to see. "Would one o'clock work okay?"

Brad nodded. "I'll be here then."

"Should I give the bowl to you then, or do you need it shipped?"

"I'll get it when we meet for lunch. I drove here since I wasn't sure how long I wanted to stay. I can work from anywhere with my current contract, so I figured I'd make the trip open-ended."

"Great!" *Calm down, Pax.*

Brad chuckled at his exuberance.

"Sorry. Caffeine combined with Madonna is apparently too much for me."

"I love how passionate you are."

Pax nearly swooned. That was definitely flirting, wasn't it?

He's straight. He's straight. Pax kept up the mantra, but his cock refused to listen.

"See you soon, Pax." Brad grinned as he walked out, closing the door behind him.

***

Cindy whistled. "Who was that?"

"That was Brad."

Her mouth dropped open. "The guy you had a crush on in high school? Why didn't you introduce me?"

One night after too much vodka, Pax had overshared with his enthusiastic young assistant. "He was just stopping by. He'll be back later. We're going to lunch, if you don't mind watching the shop."

"Mind? Of course not. You didn't tell me he was still as hot as he must have been in high school."

Pax sighed. "Actually, he's hotter."

"And you're meeting him for lunch?" Cindy fanned herself. "What are you going to wear?"

"Um…" Pax looked down at his linen shirt and khakis. "This."

"You'll have paint all over it."

"That's what the smocks are for."

She gave him a look like he'd lost his mind. "We're working with six-year-olds this morning."

Pax loved Cindy, and he wouldn't have gotten through the last couple of years without her help, but she was a huge gossip, and he did not want her thinking he was trying to turn Brad gay. "We're just catching up. You know he was Rob's best friend."

Cindy gave him a skeptical glance. "Catching up, huh?"

Madonna's "Lucky Star" faded out, and "Crazy for You" began to stream from the speakers. Cindy started singing it in a loud drunk-on-karaoke-night voice while giving Pax meaningful looks.

"Quit that!" he snapped. Her teasing was more irritating than it should have been, because clearly he *was* still crazy for Brad. He should never have asked him to lunch.

Cindy laughed. "Well, he's crazy about you, anyway."

Pax stared at her. "What?"

"Didn't you notice the way he was watching you?"

"Brad is straight," he insisted.

Cindy rolled her eyes. "Not based on what I just saw."

He glared at her, and she held up her hands in mock surrender. "I'm just telling it like I see it."

What had she seen? Surely Rob would've mentioned if Brad was gay, unless… The night Rob had died, he'd tried to tell Pax something about Brad, but he'd lost consciousness before he could finish. And he never woke up. Pax thought he'd accepted that he'd never know what Rob had tried to say. Now he wanted to know more than ever.

***

For once, Pax was thrilled that the first-grade class was as rowdy as expected. They distracted him from having a nervous breakdown about his non-date with Brad. He took the kids on a tour of the studio space, gave a demonstration on throwing pots, and they each painted a tile. When it was over, Pax was exhausted and thankful that not only Cindy, but also her friend Jada, who now worked at the gallery part-time, were there to help. By the time the last kid walked through the door, Pax needed a drink, and it was barely noon. He wouldn't have one, though, not even at lunch. He couldn't risk anything lowering his inhibitions around Brad.

Cindy sent Pax upstairs to shower and change, insisting that she and Jada would do the cleanup. She probably wanted to gossip about him, but he tried not to think about that too much. After he wrapped up the bowl Brad had bought, he headed to his apartment.

Of course Cindy had been right; he'd gotten paint on his pants and the edge of his sleeve. He stripped down and sprayed stain remover on the garments before tossing them in the laundry basket. After a quick shower, he stood staring into his closet. What should he wear? More importantly, why was he so fucking concerned about it? Brad had been in jeans and a T-shirt, and Pax doubted he would change before lunch.

Finally, he settled on his favorite jeans—the ones that were tight enough to show off that he'd more or less kept in shape, but not so tight they looked slutty—and a red T-shirt, formfitting without being overly obvious. Pax didn't want Brad to think he was trying to seduce him to his sinful ways, but if by some miracle Brad was interested, Pax wanted him to like what he saw.

He dressed, then messed around with his hair for a few minutes, using just a touch of gel, though he doubted it would hold against the August humidity.

It's just Brad.

As if that helped. Though he had seen Pax as an awkward kid. For all Pax knew, Brad still saw him as a scrawny fourteen-year-old with braces. If nothing else, maybe this lunch would erase that image for good.

Chapter Five

When Pax got back downstairs, Brad was already there, perusing the various unpainted ceramic pieces customers could choose to paint. Cindy and Jada were standing near the door of the office, stealing glances at him and giggling.

Pax caught Cindy's attention and scowled at her, but that just made her giggle harder. Ignoring her was his best course of action.

"Have you been waiting long?" he asked, walking toward Brad.

Brad turned and smiled. It was not the sort of standard polite greeting smile you might give to anyone, but rather a smile that said he was truly happy to see Pax again. "Don't worry about it, I was early. I..." He hesitated. Was that embarrassment?

Was Brad really that eager to see him again? He'd assumed Brad was just visiting out of duty more than anything.

He looked up your art. He bought the highest priced piece in the gallery. Cindy said— Stop. He's here as a friend and that's it.

"I was wondering..."

"Yes?" Pax asked when Brad seemed reluctant to continue.

"I'm usually all for trying something new, and I do want to try the sandwich shop eventually. But would you mind going to Trish's instead? I've been craving a piece of pie ever since I scheduled my trip."

Pax remembered the last time he and Brad had eaten pie together, in the tree house in his parents' backyard. It was the first time he'd laughed since Rob had died.

Brad's eyes widened. "Oh, I… I'm sorry. I didn't mean to make you think about… We can go to the sandwich shop."

Pax laid a hand on his arm, and—holy shit!—he felt the same zing that had run through him when Brad had taken his arm and guided him into the backyard after Rob's funeral. Pax had been about to lose it, and Brad was the one thing that saved him.

"No, it's fine. That… That's the one good memory I have from that week."

"It is?"

Pax nodded.

"Well, then; let's go get some pie."

"Maybe just one slice this time."

Brad laughed. "I might even be convinced to eat a sandwich first, like a civilized person."

"That might be pushing it."

"Come on. My car's right out front, so I'll drive, if that's all right."

Pax grabbed Brad's bowl for him. When they stepped outside, Brad beeped open a shiny new BMW X3. Work must be treating him very well indeed. "I love your car."

"Thanks. I wanted one for years and finally decided not to wait anymore."

Pax thought of his twelve-year-old Prius with the dent in the driver's door. He was very glad Brad was driving.

After Brad pulled out of the parking space, Pax said, "Are you still working for the same company?"

"No, I'm working for myself now."

"Oh, wow. How did you—"

They were interrupted by Brad's phone ringing from its place on the console. He glanced down as he pulled up to a red light. "I'm sorry. It's one of my clients."

"Go ahead."

The person on the other end of the line did most of the talking. Brad occasionally mentioned spreadsheets and data and used some technical jargon.

***

Trish's diner was on the outskirts of town where the two US highways that framed Ames Bridge crossed. The town being as small as it was, the drive didn't even take ten minutes. They were pulling into Trish's parking lot as he ended the call.

Brad cut the engine, and they got out of the car. As they walked to the door, Pax thought about his friends Cal and Beck and how, well before anyone *knew* they were dating, people *assumed* they were a couple when they were seen together. Of course everyone knew both of them were gay. Brad had been a jock in high school, though Cal had too for that matter. But Brad hadn't given people any reason to suspect he liked men, except for Cindy, apparently. No one would think anything of him and Brad having lunch together. He was being paranoid. Straight men went out to lunch with friends or colleagues all the time.

Still, he considered warning Brad that rumors

might get started, but that would sound ridiculous. Brad had been his brother's best friend. Of course they were going to hang out while he was here.

"Do you want to sit at a booth or a table?" Pax asked.

"Let's get one of the booths on the side. Less people are likely to stop and chat there."

"Good call."

Trish's was a popular place to learn all the latest gossip, and plenty of people liked to circulate and talk to everyone they knew. Since everybody knew everybody, that added up to a lot of chatting. Sitting in the center of the dining area would be an open invitation, but the only way Pax and Brad would be completely left alone was if they turned invisible.

Fabiana, a high-school student who'd recently started working at Trish's, came to take their drink orders.

"Sweet tea," Brad said. "I've missed it."

Pax laughed. "I bet you have."

"Tea for you too, Mr. Pax?"

"Yes, thank you."

"What are you going to order?" Brad asked when Fabiana headed toward the kitchen.

"Probably a club sandwich, but I'm not sure. Chicken and dumplings is the special today." Pax looked at the menu, which was pointless since he basically had it memorized. "What about you?"

"I can't turn down the chance for one of Trish's cheeseburgers."

Pax was about to reply when he sensed someone approaching. "Brad Watson. I haven't seen you in years."

"Miss Irene, how are you?" Brad slipped out of the booth and gave her a hug.

When one thought of town gossips, Irene, bless her heart, was at the top of that food chain.

"I was just talking to Scott about the reunion and wondering if you were coming." Her youngest son, Scott, had graduated with Brad and Rob.

Brad grinned. "I wouldn't miss it."

"How are you, Paxton?"

Irene had a thing for calling everyone by their full names, like it or not. Brad was lucky. His parents had gone for short and simple, no need for a nickname.

"I'm doing fine."

She turned back to Brad. "Did you know he's been giving me and Elsie lessons?"

Brad looked like he was fighting not to laugh, probably imagining Pax trying to get a word in edgewise as he taught them. "What kind of lessons?"

"Painting."

"Oh, I didn't know you were interested in art."

"Well, there's only so much crocheting a person can do before everything is covered in afghans. I figured I needed a new hobby, and Elsie's granddaughter and her partner had taken a class, so I thought why not."

"Well, that must be a lot of fun."

Pax nodded. "Oh yes." Truthfully, it was. They were enthusiastic, and they'd improved greatly over the last few months. He'd do well to have more students like them even if they—or at least Irene—did talk nonstop.

"You need to stop by and see me sometime,"

Irene said. "And I know Elsie will want to see you too."

"How's she doing?"

"Good as ever. She's helping her granddaughter plan her wedding."

If Irene was the Queen of Gossip, Elsie was her prime minister. The two of them were rarely seen without each other.

"Did you know Helen passed a year ago?" Irene asked.

Brad nodded. "I heard. That was too bad. Her grandson's living here now, right?"

"He sure is. He and Cal are an item now. They're getting married next spring."

"Wow! That's great news." Brad's relaxed smile showed he was truly pleased. Pax didn't think he was just being sociable.

Irene beamed. "We're all so excited. Well, those of us who are right-minded. Some people just can't accept anyone different than them."

"It's hard for me to imagine Cal being old enough to get married. I haven't seen him in years, and he was just a kid back then."

"He's…what? Ten years younger than you?" Irene asked.

"That's right," Pax interjected. "He's definitely all grown up, and he's changed a lot. You should take a tour of his farm while you're here."

"That's a great idea." Irene patted Brad's arm. "I'm so glad you're back in town, and Scott will be too. I'll tell him to give you a call."

"Thanks, Miss Irene."

"Well, I'll let you boys get back to your lunch.

You sure do make an adorable couple."

Pax sputtered as heat rushed to his face. "Oh, we're not together like that. We're—"

Brad laid a hand over Irene's where it still rested on his forearm. "Thank you. It's good to see you too." His calm tone said he wasn't the least bit concerned that she thought there was more to their lunch than two old friends catching up. Maybe Brad's views had gotten a lot more progressive since he's been living in a big city.

Pax realized Fabiana was standing close by with their drinks. She must have been waiting, not wanting to interrupt. Hopefully she didn't always do that when Irene stopped by someone's table. If she did, things would get terribly backed up in the kitchen.

Pax kept his gaze on his menu as she set the glasses on the table. "Do you know what you want?"

Brad nodded. "I'll have a cheeseburger and fries," Brad said.

"Do you want your usual, Mr. Pax?"

He looked up, still flustered from Irene's bold statement. Food. He was supposed to order food. "Yes, that's good."

At that point he didn't care what she brought. He was too busy wondering how he was going to get through an entire lunch after Irene's comments.

"Okay, I'll have that out soon."

Fabiana walked away, and Pax took a sip of his tea to further delay the need to speak. When he set his glass down, he realized Brad was watching him.

"Are you okay?"

"I'm fine. I should've warned you people

might think something. Two straight men can go to lunch here and nobody says a thing, but a gay man comes in, and suddenly he's paired up with whoever he's with no matter whether—"

Brad held up a hand. "It's fine. I promise."

Pax couldn't quite read the look on his face. He wasn't as relaxed as he'd been a few moments ago. Was he…disappointed? No, that didn't make sense.

Brad glanced around at the other diners. He seemed as uncertain about what to say next as Pax was. When the silence stretched too long, Pax fell back on the topic of Brad's job. "So you said you're working for yourself now. How did that happen?"

"I had several long-term contracts when I was at Anders-Flynn, and one of the clients asked me if I'd consider doing a project for them on my own. They'd not been thrilled with the others on my team, but they wanted my expertise. I decided to give it a go, even though it would mean putting in some crazy long hours for a while. My solution went over so well, they offered me another contract, a bigger one."

"Wow, you must've really impressed them."

Brad smiled. "Yeah, I did. I'd been thinking about looking for another job, but I'd been dicking around about it, not really wanting to put out the effort. I decided—probably way too quickly—to quit so I could freelance full-time. So far I'm happy *and* able to pay my bills."

"That's great. So you work from home?"

He chuckled. "I spend a lot of time at coffee shops, but yeah, theoretically, I work from home."

Pax glanced down at Brad's hands. No ring.

Surely Brad would've mentioned if he'd gotten married, but he figured he might as well ask. "Is it just you at home?"

Brad laughed, the same deep sound that had made Pax's cock swell as a teenager. Apparently, it still had the same effect. "Yes. The only man I've dated long-term thought marriage was far too heteronormative."

Pax's world tilted, making his head spin. "Man...? Wait. You're gay?"

Brad frowned. "Rob didn't tell you?"

The edges of Pax's vision darkened, and his heart slammed against his chest, the rhythm seemingly erratic. The words echoed in Pax's head as he slid from the booth, muttered something to Brad, and took off toward the restrooms.

Chapter Six

Pax nearly knocked over an elderly man who was coming out of the men's room as Pax went in. He ran straight into a stall and slammed the door behind him, trying to catch his breath as he fought the roiling of his stomach. When he was fairly confident he wasn't going to vomit, he sat on the toilet and pressed his hands over his eyes.

Brad probably thought he was batshit crazy, but if he'd stayed at the table, he might've passed out or thrown up or both.

Brad was gay. He thought Pax knew. He thought Rob had told him. Was that what Rob had tried to say the night he died? Pax was suddenly absolutely sure it was.

Why didn't you tell me sooner?

The only thing Rob had ever said when Pax demanded to know what happened between him and Brad was that Brad had been dishonest.

Rob had to suspect that Pax'd had a crush on Brad in high school. Why the hell hadn't he told Pax about Brad? And what did he mean by dishonest? Because he didn't tell Rob he was gay years before? Pax hadn't waited nearly as long, but it wasn't like he'd told Rob as soon as he knew himself.

Pax took a long, slow breath and glanced up at the white-and-gray-speckled drop ceiling in the diner's bathroom. *At least you tried to fix things in the end.*

Pax didn't let anyone know he occasionally talked to his dead brother. He wasn't crazy enough to expect a response, but different as they were, they'd been close, and it was hard to break the habit of sharing things with him.

Shit! He needed to go back out there and face Brad, assuming he hadn't left after Pax ran away like a loon. He washed his hands and splashed a bit of cold water on his face. Then he pushed through the swinging door and headed back toward their booth.

Brad was gone. Great. He'd run off a man he'd been crushing on for twenty years after finding out there was actually a chance for them.

But when he turned toward the side door, he saw Brad standing at the counter, holding a bag filled with takeout boxes. He had a Styrofoam cup in his other hand, and another sat on the counter next to him.

"Are you okay?" he asked when Pax reached him.

Pax nodded. "I'm sorry. I can explain, but…"

"No need unless you want to. I got our food to go. I thought you could take yours home. Or if you still want to hang out, we can go someplace quieter."

Brad's low voice soothed him. Pax didn't want to run from him, no matter how many conflicting emotions were racing through his mind. "I'd like to talk to you."

Brad grinned. "Let's go."

Pax grabbed his drink, and they walked to the car.

After Brad started the engine, he said, "I told

Trish that we started talking about Rob and the grief hit you hard. I thought that might make it easier to—"

"Thank you. I'm sure there'll be all kinds of tales flying around town about me having a breakdown, but that will help. Grief is something people understand, and actually…"

"Yes?"

"I did freak out because of Rob. In part, anyway. I… It's complicated."

"I'm willing to listen, if you want to tell me."

Pax nodded. "Let's wait until we get to wherever we're going."

"The park by the bridge? It won't be too crowded on a weekday, and we can sit at one of the tables tucked under the trees."

One of the tables couples sat at. The secluded tables. The make-out tables. "Um…yeah, that sounds great."

Brad turned onto the highway that would take them to the historic covered bridge.

Pax blew out a long breath. "I'm so sorry about running off. You must have thought—"

"It's okay. I shocked you. I really had no idea you didn't… So at the funeral you had no idea?"

"No," Pax said, wondering how long it would take to get over the shock.

"Wow. I thought…"

"What?"

Brad shook his head. "Nothing."

A few minutes later, they pulled into the parking lot. There was a large family using a few of the tables, an older couple at another, and a few teenagers unpacking their fishing rods. He and Brad could have relative privacy at one of the tables on the outskirts of the park, which was good because what Pax needed to say wasn't for anyone else to hear.

They sat on the bench and unpacked the food. He'd added a piece of pie for each of them. "Do you mind if we eat while we talk?"

Pax shook his head. It was past one thirty now, and Brad was probably starving. "No problem. I might have to eat my pie first, though."

"I won't tell anyone."

His smile had Pax sinking his teeth into his lower lip. Damn, he was gorgeous. And gay. And... Fuck.

Pax took a few bites of pie and let the sugar invigorate him. Then he tried to find the right words to explain his meltdown.

"Finding out you're gay surprised me, but what made me—" His cheeks burned. Could he really do this?

"Just talk. It's fine." Brad laid a hand on his. The contact did nothing to cool him down.

He drew in a shaky breath. "The night Rob died, I made it to the hospital just before we lost him."

"Oh, Pax. I had no idea. That must've been..."

Pax looked up at Brad and gave a weak smile. "Yeah, it was hell. He tried to tell me something, something about you, but the doctors had sedated him. He passed out before he could finish speaking. That was the last time he was conscious before we lost him."

Brad squeezed Pax's hand, and Pax squeezed

back. Brad's touch was like a lifeline. "I've wished ever since that I could figure out what he wanted to tell me. I wondered if he wanted me to apologize to you because he ignored you for so long. I thought about telling you when you were here, but without knowing for sure, I figured it might make things harder for you. Now I think I know. He was going to tell me you're gay."

Pax hated the pain he saw in Brad's eyes. "I really didn't think he'd keep that from you, but I should've guessed. It's what we argued over."

"Did he give you a hard time about it?" Rob hadn't been thrilled when Pax had come out, but he couldn't imagine Rob ending his friendship with Brad just because he liked guys.

Brad shook his head. "He didn't really mind. It was more that I'd hidden it from him."

Pax sighed. "I hid it too, but not for as long."

"The thing is, I lied to him, pretended I'd been on dates with women, made shit up about girls I liked. I'm not proud of that, and I apologized, but Rob said I'd betrayed our friendship by not being honest. If I'd known he'd be okay with it, I would've told him sooner. But it took me so damn long to accept it myself, I didn't think anyone from back home was ready to handle it."

Pax nodded. He understood. He knew plenty of guys who were in their mid-thirties like him and still hadn't told their families, despite knowing they were gay since their teens.

"He stopped speaking to me after that, and he…"

Pax grew impatient waiting for him to resume

speaking. "He what?"

"Never mind, it's—"

"Brad, tell me."

"He told me to stay away from you."

Oh my God. "Wow. I can't believe he warned you off me like I was a kid who needed protecting. Did he think you had a thing for me back in high school or something?" Had he really just suggested that Brad The Stud Watson had crushed on him back when he was a skinny teenage nerd?

"He didn't just think it; he knew it. I told him I had a crush on you. I realized how stupid that was almost as soon as I said it, but it was too late."

Whoa. Brad had wanted Pax in high school? *Don't freak out.* "I… I'm sorry he acted like that. Did you even know I was gay when you told him?"

"Yeah, I didn't need anyone to tell me."

Pax's cheeks heated as he remembered that day in his parents' basement when he, Rob, and Brad listened to the CD Julie had given Rob.

"When did you realize you liked guys?" Brad asked.

"When I was fourteen."

Brad smiled, and the tension left his face. "I think I realized it about the same time you did, then."

"Yeah?"

"There's a reason I never wrestled with you again after Christmas break my freshman year of college."

"Oh fuck! You did feel it."

Brad nodded.

Was Brad's memory of that day as clear as Pax's? Could he still feel Pax's hands against his chest, clutching for just a second too long before pushing him away? Just like Pax remembered Brad's arms closing around him, his hard thigh grazing Pax's erection, the way he smelled like sweat and Christmas cookies. Pax still got hard when he smelled snickerdoodles. How the hell was that even possible?

Brad grinned. "I felt it, and I wished I could do something about it."

"You what?" No way was this happening. Could he manage to pinch himself without Brad seeing him? "This isn't some elaborate joke, is it? Because—"

"No. I would never do something like that to you."

"I know." And he did, but it all seemed so impossible.

"When I felt your hard cock against me, I wanted to pin you under me and kiss you senseless. That's when I finally admitted to myself that I was gay."

"But you didn't say anything."

Brad looked pained. "What could I have said? 'Rob, I don't want to hear any more about Julie's enormous tits, I'm busy fantasizing about your little brother'?"

Pax laughed despite the shittiness of the situation. "I guess not."

Brad ran his hand through his hair, mussing it up. "Even though I knew then, I didn't have the courage to tell anyone else I was gay for years. I finally told my sister after college, but my parents didn't know until five years ago when I told Rob."

Silence stretched between them for the next

few moments. Pax ate a piece of pie even though he wasn't hungry anymore. He was too stunned and conflicted to savor the fruity goodness.

What could he say? Brad had admitted to wanting him in high school, and he clearly knew Pax had felt the same way. But what about now? High school was a damn long time ago.

"What made you move back to Ames Bridge?" Brad asked.

His question startled Pax out of his agonizing thoughts. It was an obvious ploy to change the uncomfortable subject of high-school crushes, but Pax was grateful for it.

"My parents weren't doing well after Rob died, and then my mom had a stroke. They needed me."

"Oh no. Is your mom okay?"

Pax nodded. "She made a full recovery except for some weakness in her left leg, but I still worry about her. I worry if she pushes herself too hard, it could happen again."

"What do the doctors say?"

"They say she'll be fine, but… I don't like to think about it."

"Then tell me about how you ended up starting your own business."

He told Brad all about the rough start with the gallery and the shop, how he built his business slowly until he had a steady stream of school groups, birthday parties, and other events. And eventually, a good number of buyers for the gallery. Then they reminisced about people from high school, several of whom still lived in Ames Bridge. The one thing they didn't mention again was their mutual attraction.

When they pulled up at the gallery so Brad could drop Pax off, Brad said, "Do you mind if I call you tomorrow?"

"I'd like that. I'll give you my number."

Brad shifted nervously. "Unless you've changed it in the last two years, I still have it. I really did intend to call you after the funeral, but once I got back to Chicago I let time pass and then I just…chickened out."

Pax nodded. "I understand. I thought about calling you too and never worked up the nerve. But call me for real this time."

Brad grinned. "I will. I'm going to be in town until Sunday at least. I'd like to see you again."

"Yeah, me too." But would he? He wanted Brad just as much as he had all those years ago. If Brad felt the same and they acted on it, what would it be like when he went back to Chicago? Even more lonely than it was now? And if Brad didn't feel the same, then Pax would just spend even more months—years?—of his life mooning over him.

Chapter Seven

Brad sank down on the bed, burying his face in the pillow. He'd told Pax he wanted him, told him about high school. Not that he'd actually promised Rob he wouldn't go after him, not that Rob had asked in a way that deserved respect, but he couldn't stop hearing Rob telling him to leave Pax alone. He hadn't even told Pax that Brad had come out. Why should Brad care about what Rob had wanted?

Because Pax is Rob's brother, and you were Rob's best friend for years.

But he and Pax were alive, and they shouldn't throw away something both of them had obviously wanted for a long time. Until two years ago, Brad had figured that his crush on Pax was just a high-school thing he remembered fondly. Then he had seen Pax again, and all those feelings came rushing back, not to mention merely touching his arm set off sparks.

And the way Pax's eyes had darkened and his cheeks had turned red when Brad brought up that wrestling match… He still felt something too.

Part of the reason Brad had come back was to reconcile with his past: his memories of Rob, his memories of high school, of not being who he really was.

But now that he was here, it felt like high school all over again. Just telling Pax he remembered that day had felt like it took as much courage as diving off a cliff or jumping out of a plane, things he'd done to prove to himself that he was brave even if he couldn't tell his family he was gay. And then he'd found a good therapist who helped him work through how he was feeling without the need for dangerous and expensive pursuits, not that he regretted those experiences. He was glad he'd had them, but he didn't need that constant rush now.

Or at least he'd thought he didn't. Now that he was back in Ames Bridge with the prospect of seeing Scott and all the other guys he'd hung out with, that critical voice inside him screamed for him to do something big, something to prove how brave he was, but it was nearly drowned out by the urge to get in his car and drive back to Chicago as fast as he could.

But he had something big he needed to do here—come out. And it was scarier than any cliff dive. It was important, though. He needed to go to the reunion as the man he actually was, not the misimpression people had from high school.

But after less than a day in town, he wasn't sure he could ever be himself here. And if he couldn't, there wasn't a real chance with Pax. He owned a gallery, a successful one. He wasn't just going to up and leave town because of an old crush.

Whoa. Brad was really getting ahead of himself. For all he knew, Pax was just humoring him by agreeing to go out again. And it wasn't like their lunch had actually been a date. But Pax had admitted to returning his interest, and Brad had caught him letting his gaze drop to Brad's lips, watching them move. Pax wanted him, and Brad was determined to make that happen. Once he decided to do something, he went all in. He'd always been that way. Sometimes it was great, like when he didn't hesitate to jump from a plane, or when, years ago, he marched right into the company he wanted to work for and told them why he was perfect for one of their openings. But other times, more thinking and less jumping was best. Yet he wanted to jump into something with Pax. Hell, he just plain wanted to jump Pax.

With a sigh, he pushed himself to a sitting position. Lying around feeling sorry for himself wasn't doing him any good. But what else was there to do? Had he thought Ames Bridge had suddenly become a bastion of entertainment possibilities? He could call one of his old friends, but they were likely at work, and he'd had only minimal contact with them over the last several years, just the occasional 'like' of one of their Facebook posts or a Happy Birthday comment. He could visit Irene, but he wasn't quite sure he was up to that.

He sighed. Other than the women's Bible study his mom had always participated in, he couldn't think of anything to do on a Wednesday afternoon—Wait, the tailgate market. Did that still happen on Wednesdays? Maybe he could look around, pick up some peaches or berries and a bouquet for Irene. At least if he sat with her for a while, he'd be caught up on all the town gossip.

***

The market was located on the edge of town, not far from Trish's diner. It was crowded that afternoon, but Brad managed to find a parking spot on the grass near the back of the makeshift lot. Before he even reached the rows of booths, he'd already been stopped three times by people he knew. Maybe it wasn't going to be that easy to actually shop. How did people get anything done when they all knew each other and half of them talked like it was a competitive sport?

As he scanned the booths, looking for berries and flowers, he managed not to make eye contact with a group of his mother's friends from the First Methodist church. He supposed he'd have to get more skilled at that if he stayed long. Was he actually thinking about staying? And what? Basing his consulting business from Ames Bridge?

Oh, shit, there was Marcie Nelson or whatever her last name was now. She'd been his graduating class's stereotypical mean girl. Maybe he'd been wrong about everyone being at work; apparently they were all here at the market.

Finally, he saw some beautiful blackberries. He was debating how many he needed when a man said, "The berries were just picked this morning. The quart baskets are two for fourteen dollars."

Brad looked up, and—holy shit—was that Cal McMurtry all grown up?

"Brad?"

"Yes. Cal, right?"

"Yep." Cal gestured toward a blond man who'd just finished ringing up a sale. "That's my partner, Beck. He used to spend part of the summer here when we were kids."

"Oh yes, Helen Stone's grandson."

"Guilty as charged," Beck said, stepping over to join them.

Damn, they made an attractive couple. "So

y'all are working together now?"

Beck grinned. "He's determined to make a farmer out of me, but I also have an event-planning business. I'm working with Pax on an art show. He mentioned you were going to be in town."

"For the reunion," Cal chimed in.

Damn, they even finished each other's sentences. Fighting the urge to stare, Brad looked back down at the berries.

"You should get some," Beck said. "They're the best."

"I will. And one of the bouquets too."

"A gift for someone?" Beck grinned.

Cal cleared his throat. "You don't need to go turning into a matchmaker."

Beck's eyes widened. "Did I imply that?"

"Beckett."

Heat filled Brad's cheeks. "They're for Miss Irene, actually. She asked me to stop by."

"Be sure you have a few hours before you do. I bet she's got a gazillion questions for you."

Brad laughed. "I'm sure she does."

"Are you going to this reunion prom thing they're having?" Beck asked.

Cal wrinkled his nose in disgust. "A what?"

"Someone"—Brad paused as he thought of Martin, the obnoxious former student government president—"it's probably best I don't know exactly who, thought it would be a great idea to recreate our prom as part of our twentieth reunion weekend."

Cal snorted. "A bunch of grown-ups going to prom."

"With a Cowboy Hoedown theme."

Cal winced.

Beck gave his arm a mock punch. "It could be fun."

"It could be hell." Cal was not wrong.

"I haven't decided whether to go or not."

"You should," Beck said. "I bet Pax would be happy to go with you."

Brad sputtered. Maybe his gayness wasn't such a secret after all; first Irene and now Beck.

Cal gave Beck a warning look. "Don't mind him."

Brad had considered asking Pax, but the whole thing was so cheesy and they'd have to deal with all his friends and their reactions to him bringing a man to the prom/reunion. Pax didn't deserve that. "Um… I haven't…"

"Don't let him pressure you," Cal said.

"Where would you be if you'd taken that attitude?"

Cal scowled at Beck. "Nobody pressured me into going after you."

"Ha!"

"They gave me a push. I did the rest."

Beck turned back to Brad. "We're getting married next spring."

"I heard. Congratulations."

"Thanks."

A few more customers came into the tent, and Brad decided he'd best make his escape before Beck had him engaged to Pax. That thought sent an unexpected surge of heat through him. Did he want to be engaged? No, that was getting *waaay* ahead of himself.

"Where's the best place to get peaches?" he asked Cal. "Or am I too late in the season?"

"Sumner's Farm has some great late-season varieties. They're across the way a few booths down."

Brad turned and looked where Cal was pointing.

"See the kid with the dark hair? That's Luke Sumner, Trish's nephew."

"The one who almost died when he was a baby?" That had happened right after Brad graduated.

Cal nodded. "Yeah, he just turned twenty-one, and he's healthy as can be."

"He looks it." Brad realized how wrong that sounded as soon as the words were out of his mouth, but Cal just chuckled.

"He sure does."

Beck raised his brows. "Does he now?"

Brad grinned at Beck's mock scowl. "Thanks, y'all. I'll see you later."

"Come out to the farm before you leave town," Cal said. "We'll give you a tour."

"I'd like that. Pax told me you'd really changed the place."

Cal nodded. "You'll be shocked."

As Brad crossed to the Sumner's Farm booth, he studied Luke. He couldn't imagine being seriously interested in anyone that young, but damn, Luke was hot. He had wavy hair that begged to have fingers run through it and that country-boy-who-was-up-for-anything look. Brad bet he was the subject of a hell of a lot of teen fantasies.

He'd been born with a severe heart defect. When complications arose after an initial surgery, his doctors hadn't expected him to live, but Trish had one of her famous "feelings" he was going to be just fine. To this day, she and Luke's parents swore the love he got from their large family—basically the rest of the town—was what kept him alive until he could have a second surgery. Even then, the doctors thought he'd never be able to be active, but he proved everyone wrong. Brad could tell by his sculpted arms and bulky shoulders that he was still going strong.

Brad stepped into his booth, and Luke looked up. Wow. Add beautiful blue eyes and freckles to his list of attributes.

"Can I help you?" he asked.

"Yeah, Cal told me this was the place to get some peaches."

Luke grinned as he gestured to the counter in front of him. "We've got plenty."

Brad looked down at the baskets of peaches and heat crept up his neck. He hadn't even seen what was right in front of him because he'd been too busy eyeing Luke.

"I'll take two baskets, one for me and one for Miss Irene."

"Hoping she'll make you a pie?"

Brad laughed. "I wouldn't mind that, but she asked me to stop by. Her son Scott and I were close in school, and she wants to hear all about how my parents are doing."

"She'll love these. Are those flowers for her too?"

Brad nodded. "You wouldn't remember me, but I'm Brad Watson. I'm back for—"

"The reunion. And sure; you were a big

football star. I've seen your name on the trophies. You're one of the ones Coach J talks about all the time because you were a good student *and* a strong player."

"Damn, I hope he's not using my record to make everyone feel guilty."

"Nah, not really," Luke said. "He's a good guy. He just wanted us all to do our best."

Jeff Johnson, a.k.a Coach J, was two years older than Brad. He'd been captain of the team the first year Brad played varsity. "He was good at encouraging all of us back when we played together."

"I bet. You need anything else?" Luke asked.

Brad shook his head.

"Okay. That will be ten dollars."

Brad handed him a ten and studied the other produce in the booth as Luke rang up the sale and put the baskets of peaches in a small box to make them easier to carry. When Brad turned back, he caught Luke staring at him. Luke turned away quickly and started fiddling with a stack of paper bags. Well, that was certainly interesting.

"It was good to see you."

"You too," Luke stammered. "Um…enjoy the peaches."

Brad smiled. "I will."

As he walked to his car, his phone rang. He didn't recognize the number, but it was a local one, so he answered.

"Brad, it's Scott Tregar. My mom told me to give you a call."

Of course she did. "I was just thinking about stopping by to visit her."

"Oh, she's got her church circle dinner tonight, but I know she'd love to see you another time."

"I'll visit tomorrow, then," Brad said.

"You got plans tonight?"

Brad hesitated. He didn't, but he also wasn't sure he'd be up for whatever Scott proposed.

You came here to see all these people, not to sit in your quaintly decorated room at the Bridge Motel.

What if Pax… No, they'd already had lunch, and he'd said he'd call Pax tomorrow.

"Nope."

"You do now. I'm going to round up some more of the guys, and we're going to Pedro's and then out drinking."

"Oh, that sounds…" Nightmarishly like high school. "Great."

At least now he could get a margarita to help him forget that the food at Pedro's was barely half a step above Taco Bell. How were they even still in business?

"Meet us at seven?"

Brad glanced at his watch. It was five thirty, and all he needed to do was put Irene's flowers in some water and change. "Sure."

"Perfect. It will be just like old times."

Why had Brad ever thought he wanted anything to be like old times? "See you then."

He'd come back to Ames Bridge to make peace with who he'd been in high school, who Rob had been, the fact that he'd lost Rob's friendship by not being himself, by being scared. The night might suck, but it would be a good opportunity to tell his former friends that he wasn't who they thought he was.

Chapter Eight

When Brad stepped into Pedro's, he might as well have been in a time machine. Nothing seemed to have changed in twenty years. Not the booths, not the wall decor. He glanced toward the bar. Wow. Not the bartender either apparently; at least, he thought that was Oscar, one of the owners. Maybe it was his son.

A hostess materialized. She had to be new since she looked all of fourteen, though he assumed she was a bit older.

"How many?"

Brad frowned. "I'm not sure exactly. I'm meeting some people."

"Mr. Tregar and his friends?"

"Yes."

"They're toward the back."

Where they could get loud and drunk and obnoxious. Perfect. "I'll find them."

"Are you sure?"

He nodded.

She handed him a menu, and he began to make his way through the noisy restaurant. His chest felt constricted as he attempted a last deep breath before having to face his "friends." This was one night. If it was that bad, he could bail on the rest of the reunion activities. Tonight he would sit down and be himself, not the confused kid he'd been when he hung out with these guys.

When he turned into what used to be the smoking section of the restaurant, he saw Scott. Seated with him were Jack, who'd been quiet and easy-going, and Troy, the worst of the lot and the most homophobic.

"Brad!" Scott jumped up and pulled him into a back-slapping bro hug as soon as he reached the table.

Before he could recover from being nearly squeezed to death, the other guys jumped in, taking their turns.

"Wow, you're looking good, man," Scott said. "Tell us all about the big city."

Brad wasn't sure what to say. "It's great except when it's freeze-your-balls-off cold in January and February."

Troy grimaced. "You really don't mind all those people crowding you in?"

"Nope, there's so much to see and interesting people, and I can walk or take the train most places I want to go."

Troy took a swig of beer. "I wouldn't want to live anywhere I can't drive my truck."

Brad shrugged. "You might like it better than you think."

"Nah, man, all those weirdoes and liberals."

Ah yes, those. Queers too. "I like the diversity. So where are you all living now?"

Troy looked at him like he was crazy. "Here, man."

"All of you?"

They nodded.

"You still work at your father's firm?" he asked Troy.

"Sure do."

Scott snorted. "When he works."

"So I fish when I get a chance. I get my clients off. That's all that matters."

Troy was a personal-injury lawyer. Last time Brad had been in town, he'd even seen Troy's face on a billboard. Brad was fairly sure most of Troy's success was more a result of money his family donated to the campaigns of several local judges than any skill of his own.

He didn't need to hear more about Troy's poor work ethic, so he turned to Scott. "Are you running Tregar Accounting now?"

"I am. I took over after my dad died."

"And things are good?"

"Yeah, I just hired a new accountant."

"Jack's the only one that didn't follow in his father's footsteps," Troy said.

Jack took a sip of his beer and studiously ignored Troy. His father had been their football coach, and it was no secret he'd wanted Jack to teach and coach like he had.

"You were living in Greensboro the last time we talked, right?" Brad asked Jack, hoping to change the subject.

"I was. I worked at a hotel there for years, but now I run a bed-and-breakfast out by the bridge."

"He bought the old Johnson place and fixed it up real nice," Scott added.

"Oh, right. I heard about that," Brad said. "It's doing well, isn't it?"

That brought a smile to Jack's face. "This summer's been great. We're getting a lot more tourists now."

"Yeah, McMurtry got his farm on some fancy tour circuit," Troy added. "People come to see it, and Helen Stone's place is now one of them Airbnbs."

"You know Cal McMurtry's gay now, right?" Scott took a sip of his beer before continuing. "He and Miss Helen's grandson are living together right there on his family farm."

He was quite sure Cal had always been gay but had chosen not to tell anyone until recently. And where else should he and Beck live? "I saw them at the farmers' market today. They looked really happy."

Troy snorted. "They got caught fucking in the barn."

"Troy, that's enough." Jack's tone was surprisingly sharp. "Cal's done a lot with his farm, and it's good for all of us in town to have him bringing in visitors."

"Don't mind him." Troy waved a dismissive hand toward Jack. "He gets to profit from it. And he's Episcopalian anyway. They tolerate all that gay shit."

"You tolerate it just fine when it's hog-slaughter season and you want some of Cal's pork," Jack pointed out.

"Well, his parents are good people."

Jack nodded. "Good people who support him."

"He's their son. I mean, yeah, it's gross, but everybody's got some shit in their family."

Tell them.

Now was the right time. The longer he put it off, the harder it would get.

His pulse whooshed in his ears. He realized Scott was saying something, but he didn't hear it.

Tell them.

Not yet.

They ordered, and when the food came, Brad was pleased to discover it had improved some. It wasn't excellent, but clearly the cook was one of the few updates.

"You married?" Scott asked, glancing at his left hand.

Brad shook his head.

"Divorced?" This from Troy.

"No, just never found anyone to settle down with."

Troy snorted. "You and Jack've got the right idea. I've been married twice. Bitches, both of them."

After a few seconds of awkward silence, Scott said, "Melanie and I just had our fifteenth anniversary. There are some good ones out there."

Brad smiled. Scott could be a bastard, but he'd loved Melanie since high school. "Congratulations."

"Thanks."

As they finished their food, they mostly talked about what other members of their class were up to. A depressing number of them were living the same lives their parents had, right there in Ames Bridge.

When the waitress asked if he'd like another margarita, Brad declined. The tequila was the kind that started to give you a headache before you took the first sip.

"You're not stopping with one, surely?" Scott asked.

"Nah, but I'm more in the mood for beer I

think."

"Hey, we should move this party to the Get Down."

Oh boy. The Get Down—the bar where good Christian boys went to act like spawns of Satan. Just where Brad wanted to go.

"You in?" Scott looked at Brad.

"Um…" Brad glanced at Jack, hoping in vain that he might protest.

Jack just shrugged.

"Yeah, sure."

Just like in high school, Jack was going along with the crowd. At least he seemed happy about his job. Brad remembered him as being well-organized and considerate of others, so running an inn seemed to fit him, even if it was hard to imagine him talking a lot with the customers.

A few hours and several games of pool later, Brad had lost count of how many beers he'd downed to cope with the bullshit he heard spouted around him by his friends and people at other tables. He'd tried twice more to work up the nerve to tell them he was gay himself, but he couldn't get the words out.

Troy returned from the bar and plunked down a tray of shots in the middle of the table.

"Who's joining me?"

Scott shook his head. "I've got to work tomorrow."

"Same here," Jack said.

Brad frowned. Doing shots with Troy was a terrible idea, but he was tired of trying to make conversation with them when he'd rather be with Pax.

Three rounds later, the room was spinning,

and Brad realized he needed to get the fuck out of there before he spilled his secrets and then got the shit beat out of him.

"Wow," Scott said. "I don't even remember seeing you that drunk in high school."

"Don't think I ever was." Back then he'd needed to stay sober enough to keep his friends from finding out he had no interest in their tales about seducing girls.

"I bet you're missing Rob a lot, aren't you?" Jack asked.

Brad nodded, even though that wasn't why he'd decided to drown out...well, everything.

"No wonder you wanted to get drunk."

"Too bad he couldn't be here." Troy's words were slurred. "Though I never understood what you saw in a nerd like him."

Had he actually said that?

"Don't talk about the dead like that," Scott scolded.

"Rob was a good guy," Jack wavered in front of Brad. Was he that unsteady, or was Brad's vision fucked?

"His little brother's a butt fucker too."

Pax. They were talking about Pax. "Don't go there," Brad snarled. "Just don't."

"Whoa." Scott grabbed his arm. "Troy's just joking around. I guess Pax was like your brother too."

No, not exactly.

"We all thought Pax and Cal would hook up," Troy nearly knocked over Scott's beer as he waved his hands around. "Probably they did, but they were just discra...disco...discreet."

Jack gave Troy a look of disgust. "Don't try those big words, Troy. They're not for you."

Brad liked Jack. A lot. The others, not so much. If Troy made one more comment about Pax, Brad was going to deck him. He would have already, except then the whole bar would erupt in a massive fight, and Troy would... What?

Know Brad for who he was? His heart pounded. *Tell them.*

"I..." They all turned to look at him. "I should go."

Jack grabbed his arm as he turned to walk off. "You can't drive like that."

Brad shook his head and then swallowed against the nausea that rose from the movement. Yeah, he was done. "I'm gonna call somebody."

"We ain't got no fancy car service here," Troy said. "My cousin's gonna come get us in a little while."

He pulled free of Jack's hold and dug his cell phone out of his pocket as he headed down the hall toward the restrooms. Thank God it was quieter there.

He scrolled through his contacts and tapped on Pax's number.

***

Pax lay on the bed, tossing and turning, wishing he could fall asleep. Irene and Elsie were coming for painting lessons in the morning, and he needed to be wide awake if he was going to deal with all their energy.

But every time he closed his eyes, he replayed the conversation he'd had with Brad. Would Brad really call again? Did Pax want him to? What would be the point? Brad lived in Chicago. Pax was basically married to the gallery, so he didn't really have time for a relationship.

Pax checked the time again. 12:30. Ugh. He tried counting backward from a thousand. That sometimes helped his mind slow down enough to let him sleep. Nothing. As his mind kept going back over every word Brad had said at lunch, "Open Your Heart" kept playing in the background. Maybe he needed to just listen to that damn song so he could get it out of his head. He put in his headphones, but after only a few lines, an incoming call superseded the lyrics.

It was Brad. What was he doing calling now? Pax's heart raced as he answered the call.

"Heeyyy, Pax!" Brad's voice was overly loud, and Pax could hear music and chatter in the background.

"What's going on, Brad? It's—"

"Pax?"

"Yes."

"I missed you." The words were slurred.

Oh, great. "You're drunk."

"I am. I'm *reeeeally* drunk. I haven't been this drunk…like this in years, maybe decades."

"Do you need me to come pick you up?" Pax figured that was likely why he was calling. Getting an Uber in Ames Bridge was about as likely as riding home on a unicorn.

"Troy Anderson—you remember him?—he said his cousin would come get us."

"Yeah." Troy had shown some promise in high school, but he'd ended up getting a law degree from a shitty party school and coming back home to work at his father's firm. He'd also followed in his father's footsteps by becoming a bigoted son-of-a-bitch who served as a church deacon on Sundays while the rest of the week he drank too much and abused his wife, or he had until she'd left him. "Let me come get you. That will be better."

"You don't have to—"

"I want to." He didn't exactly, but he wasn't leaving Brad to Troy's tender mercies. Not when he was this out of it.

"O-okay. I don't think he's my kind of guy."

Pax sighed. "No, he's not. Where are you?"

"The Get Down."

Great. A redneck bar in a part of town Pax would rather avoid. How had Brad ended up there? "Don't order anything else. I'll be there in fifteen minutes."

"No. No more drinkin'. I cut myself off. Everything's spinning."

Pax rolled his eyes. "Just stay put. I'll be there soon."

So much for trying to sleep. Pax pulled on some jeans and a T-shirt, then topped that with some invisible armor, because no way in hell was he getting out of that bar without hearing at least a few fag jokes.

Chapter Nine

Brad was waiting for Pax at the side door of the bar. Pax pulled up to the curb and got out. When Brad took a step, he swayed and stumbled. Pax hurried toward him and wrapped an arm around his waist, barely succeeding in keeping him upright.

"Didn't want you to have to go in. Not a good place for you."

Pax appreciated that but had to ask. "Why the hell were you here?"

"Troy and Scott and Jack. Wanted me to go drinking."

"Right. Let's get you to the car."

Brad moved slowly, and Pax's heart pounded, waiting for one of Brad's friends to step out and see them together. Then the name-calling would start. Most days he got along fine, but he knew where he wasn't welcome. He'd just as soon walk into Oak Baptist in the middle of a revival than go in the Get Down. Didn't Brad have any sense? Unless... "None of them know, do they?"

"Who know what?"

"Hang on." He managed to get Brad folded into his Prius.

He circled around, got into the driver's seat, and started the engine. But before he could put it in gear, Brad reached over and laid a hand on his thigh. Despite the fact that Brad smelled like a brewery and was too drunk to stand up straight, Pax's cock reacted to the warmth of his touch. This wasn't a date. Brad was likely too drunk to do anything anyway. Pax was just his designated driver.

"Who?" Brad asked. Pax was surprised he remembered the thread of conversation.

"Troy and them. They don't know you're gay."

"Started to tell them. Wanted to. But I'm a fucking coward."

Pax laid his hand over Brad's. "No, you're not. And this isn't the place to do it."

"Then where is?"

That wasn't a question Pax could answer. "Where are you staying?"

"The Bridge Motel." He laughed far louder than was necessary. "Wanted real Ames Bridge flavor this trip. Too many tourists. Shoulda just stayed at the Han-Hal-Hampton."

After a few moments of silence as Pax drove down the nearly empty streets, Brad said, "They're wrong."

Now it was Pax's turn to ask. "Who?"

"Those idiots back there." He tapped the window and pointed as if the bar was still right there. "Probably think I got so drunk 'cause I miss your brother."

Pax wasn't sure he wanted to hear where this was going. "You didn't?"

"No. I miss him, and it's weird being around people from high school and knowing he's not going to show up."

"Yeah, sometimes I still expect him to call or

show up at my parents' house."

Brad nodded.

More silence. Pax pondered asking him why he got so drunk if it wasn't about Rob, but he wasn't sure Brad could give a cogent answer.

"Hey, did you know most of my *friends*"—he put air quotes around the word—"are assholes?"

Pax chuckled. "Yeah."

"That's not why I got drunk either. Well, maybe a little. I did get tired of their shit. Troy's shit mostly. Scott held back, and Jack's not so bad."

"No, he's not. I should show you his inn while you're here."

"Yeah, you should. You should show me *everything*."

Pax swallowed hard.

"Know why I did it?" Brad asked.

"W-why?" Pax was suddenly afraid he wouldn't like the answer.

"Because I wished I was out with you."

Pax swerved, nearly going off the road. "What?"

"You know why I really came to this reunion?" The words weren't slurred. He sounded almost sober.

Pax squeezed the wheel so hard, his hands hurt. "I don't know, do I?"

"It sure as fuck wasn't to relive my glory days or to see all those assholes I used to be friends with. I needed an excuse to see you."

Butterflies turned somersaults in Pax's stomach. "Y-you did?"

"So many times I thought about coming here

just to visit you, but I couldn't get up the nerve to call you. I didn't know what to say, what you thought of me. I was afraid you were angry that I hadn't called right after the funeral, or that you might think I was a self-centered asshole like those friends of mine that—"

"Brad, I wasn't angry about that. I understood. And I never thought you were like those guys. No matter how fucking gorgeous you are, I would never have liked you if you were that big of an asshole."

The tension in the car was thicker than the August air as Pax turned onto the highway that would take them to the Bridge Motel.

Brad reached out and took hold of Pax's right hand, tugging it off the wheel. "Will you go to the prom with me?"

"What?" Maybe Brad was even more drunk than he'd thought. Was he delusional?

Brad laid his head back against the seat and closed his eyes. Then he started to laugh. A small chuckle at first, then harder, until he made a strangled noise. "Pull over."

Pax hit the brakes hard and slid onto the shoulder. Brad shoved the door open and was violently sick on the grass at the edge of the road.

Pax got out of the car, dug around in the trunk, and came up with a towel, one he used to cushion artwork he was bringing to the gallery. Brad took it and wiped his mouth.

"Thank you," he said, his voice so low Pax barely heard him. He was ghostly pale and sweating.

"Are you okay?"

"Yeah," he croaked. "Better now."

"Here." Pax reached into the console and pulled out a container of mints. "Have one of these."

Brad took one, then curled up as much as a man his size could in the seat of a small car and closed his eyes.

Neither of them spoke as Pax drove the rest of the way to the motel. When he pulled into a space in the small lot, Brad finally opened his eyes and looked at him. In them, Pax saw fear and the same vulnerability he'd seen earlier that day.

Pax reached over and squeezed his hand. "Did you really ask me to prom earlier?"

Brad nodded and then groaned. "Remind me not to move again."

"You need to drink some water and take something before you go to bed."

"Yeah. Something. Bed."

"The prom?" Pax asked again.

"They're recreating our senior prom on Saturday night, Cowboy Hoedown theme and everything."

"Seriously?" Pax remembered Rob wearing a cowboy hat and bolero with his tux when he went to prom. Pax had laughed. A lot.

Despite his intention not to move, Brad reached for Pax's hand again. "Come with me. Please."

Pax had hated prom in high school and certainly never thought he'd attend another one or anything similar, though he supposed an art auction at the country club wasn't all that different. Same type of assholes, just older and richer. Did he dare let himself get more involved with Brad? "I'm not sure that's a good idea, especially since you're not out to your friends."

"I don't give a fuck that everyone will know I'm gay. I would have told them tonight, but…"

Pax's heart thumped against his ribs, and he pulled his hand free. "I don't want you using me to make a statement."

Brad shook his head, then instantly looked green. "I wanted to ask you twenty years ago."

Pax moved his mouth, but no sound came out. Finally he forced through a "What?"

"I would much rather have taken you to the prom than Shelly Archer. She was nice enough, but I didn't like her the way she wanted me to. She kissed me afterward and offered more. When I turned her down, she got so angry, she didn't speak to me again for the rest of the year. What was I supposed to tell her? That I'd really wanted to ask my best friend's brother?"

Pax couldn't breathe. The world was going fuzzy at the edges. "Brad, I…"

"Please come with me. We can even get them to play Madonna."

Pax imagined the two of them in cowboy hats, dancing to eighties and nineties music. What the hell would Rob have thought of that? "Gay cowboys go to the prom? It sounds like bad porn."

Brad laughed. "Do you have a cowboy hat?"

"Hell, yeah," Pax responded, playing up his accent.

"Then you're coming with me."

Pax had attended a cowboy-themed fundraiser the year before and bought a full Western costume for the occasion. He could wear a dress shirt and slacks and use the hat, boots, and the vest to complete the look. No way in hell was he wearing chaps to a mock prom, but wearing them for Brad in private might be fun.

No. He wasn't going to think about that. Because Brad was leaving in a few days, and Pax would be alone again. Even if they kept in touch, it wasn't like they could have a real relationship when they were eight hundred miles apart. He'd spent enough time wishing things had been different between them.

Except now there was actually a chance for something, not just a fantasy. Even if it was only a night or two, wouldn't that be worth it?

Once Brad outed himself by taking Pax as his date, the whole town would know. And then anyone who wasn't busy trying to pray them straight would tease Pax relentlessly, even after Brad had been gone for months.

"Pax, tell me what you're thinking."

He realized he'd left Brad hanging for far too long. "What do you think will happen if we go to the prom?"

Brad grinned. "Are you worried about your virtue? Do you think I expect you to put out if I take you to prom?"

Heat filled Pax's face as he imagined Brad's powerful body over his, his warm skin sliding against Pax's as they grew slick with sweat from their exertions. His cock started to swell. "Um…not exactly."

Brad reached up and cupped his face. "Tell

me what you want?"

A gut-wrenchingly honest answer slipped out before he could stop it. "You. I've always wanted you."

"Then let's see what happens."

"But you live in Chicago."

He sighed. "A date with no pressure. That's all I'm asking."

"A date in front of some of the most gossipy people in town, a town I still live in."

Brad nodded. "Okay, I'm asking a lot. Our going together will make a statement, but in Chicago I haven't hidden who I am in years, and I don't want to do it here either."

"They won't just talk about you being gay. You were my brother's best friend. They'll speculate about your relationship with him and about what might have happened between you and me back in high school."

Brad blew out a harsh breath and laid his head against the seat. "I hadn't thought about that. Do you think Rob would've cared, if he'd ever forgiven me for not telling him I was gay?"

Pax squeezed Brad's hand. "I'm sure he forgave you. He just didn't know how to say it. You know he wasn't good at talking about feelings."

Brad nodded. "Yeah."

"He was only upset because you meant so much to him. He wouldn't have cared what those idiots said."

Brad looked at him, and Pax felt like Brad was seeing deep inside him in a way no one else ever had. "Do *you* care?"

Pax pondered his question for several seconds. "I shouldn't, but sometimes it's hard to forget how much their teasing used to hurt."

"I hated when they picked on you."

"I know. The way you defended me back then made me want you even more."

"Please come with me."

Pax sighed. "I only went to my own senior prom as a favor to a friend."

"All the better to enjoy it now."

Pax wasn't sure how enjoyable it would be, even with Brad by his side. "Will it be fun?"

Brad huffed. "I'm insulted. I'm an excellent prom date."

"Of course you are: most popular guy in school, captain of the football team, swim-team star."

He grinned. "Damn right."

"I'll be the envy of the school. Of course they'll all think I blew you for the privilege."

Brad's eyes sparkled as if he liked that idea very much. "My feelings for you haven't changed since I was eighteen. You know the day I was talking about, when we wrestled?"

Pax nodded, unable to speak as he waited to find out what else Brad had to reveal.

"I'd never been with another guy, but somehow I knew kissing you would be perfect. If only we'd been alone…" He shook his head. "Now I feel like a fucking perv. You were so damn young then."

Pax couldn't breathe, couldn't think. "You were still young too. I just can't believe I ran from you that day. I wanted exactly what you did."

"I wish you'd told me. If not that day, then…sometime in the last twenty years."

Pax rolled his eyes. "Like I was going to confess to the captain of the football team that I fantasized about him."

Brad looked at him, lust clear in his eyes. "Do you still?"

"Brad," Pax warned him. This wasn't the time to start confessing his sexual fantasies, not with Brad still drunk.

Brad closed his eyes, took a long, slow breath. "I'm sorry. It's just that after all this time, my feelings for you are still so intense. How can that be?"

"I don't know, but I feel the same way."

He looked at Pax pleadingly. "Then—"

"I'll go with you." How could he resist when he'd wanted Brad for so long?

"Thank you."

His heart would be crushed when Brad left. Because he knew how it would go. Brad would take him to bed, and the next day Pax would be left with nothing more than a wilted corsage. "What time do you want to pick me up?"

"There's a dinner beforehand, but…I'd rather just go out with you."

"I'll get us reservations. You still obsessed with seafood?"

Brad smiled. "I love that you remember what I like."

"I remember everything about you." How often had he wished he could forget?

"I'm hoping you'll learn some new things while I'm here."

Pax shivered. So did he.

Brad reached for the door handle. "Thanks for the ride."

"Do you need me to walk you to your room?" Pax didn't want him falling on his face in the motel parking lot.

"No, I'm okay. But, um…"

"Yeah?"

"You know how you mentioned a tour of Cal's farm?"

Pax nodded.

"I saw him today, and he invited me out there. I was thinking if you had time…"

Pax had already agreed to a date. He might as well see as much of Brad as he could while he was in town. "I'll call him and see if we can come out there in the late afternoon tomorrow. I don't have any lessons or groups after three, and Cindy can mind the gallery for me then."

"Good. Just text me. And I'm looking forward to prom, way more than in high school."

"Me too." Pax truly was, despite the idiots they'd encounter. A grown-up cowboy prom would be good for one or two or a hundred laughs, even if his heart would be in tatters when Brad left town.

Brad opened his door and stood. Then he leaned against the side of the car and brought a hand to his forehead. "Is the world spinning, or is it me?"

Pax laughed. "Stay right there. I'm coming."

He helped Brad to his room, then sent him to the bathroom to get some water and take some ibuprofen. He didn't want to leave without saying goodbye, so he looked around the room as he waited.

Brad had unwrapped that bowl of Pax's he'd bought, and put it on the dresser. Seeing it there made him warm all over.

When Brad stepped out of the bathroom, Pax moved toward the door. Brad was still drunk, and no matter how inviting the large bed looked, Pax wasn't sleeping with him when he was still tipsy.

"You leaving?" Brad asked, walking toward him until he stood just inches away.

"Yeah, I've got to work in the morning. I should try to get at least a little sleep." It was nearly two a.m.

"Okay." Brad sounded disappointed.

Pax started to open the door, but Brad leaned forward, trapping Pax between his arms. "Can I kiss you?" he asked. "I brushed my teeth."

Pax couldn't help but smile at his reassurance. His gaze dropped to Brad's lips. He wanted to taste him like he'd dreamed of doing for years, but this wasn't the right time. It now seemed inevitable that they would do a lot more than kiss, that finally after who knew how many jerk-off sessions where he imagined it, he would be able to feel Brad sink deep inside him.

"Tomorrow," he said, his voice breathless.

Brad closed his eyes, nodded, and stepped back.

Pax reached behind him, fumbling for the doorknob. He had to get out of there fast. Or he *was* going to kiss Brad, and he wasn't going to stop there.

"Good night," Pax said; the words echoed in the still room.

He didn't wait for Brad to respond. He rushed

out like he was being chased. When he reached his car, he plopped into the driver's seat and sat there trying to breathe as he worked to sort out the various arguments running through his brain, which ranged from "you're insane for agreeing to go out with him" to "I can't believe you didn't stay and fuck him."

A few minutes later, he looked at the clock. 2:15. A massive headache was building behind his eyes, and his hands were shaking, but he managed to drive to his building and drag himself upstairs. He fell into bed still dressed, and while he was even more worried about the situation with Brad than he'd been earlier that night, he was now so exhausted, he sank immediately into sleep.

Chapter Ten

When Pax's alarm woke him after less than four hours of sleep, he decided the entire night had been a crazy dream. Then he noticed he was on top of the covers rather than under them, and he was wearing jeans.

He rolled to his back and stared at the ceiling. *Did I really agree to go to a cowboy-themed prom hosted by a bunch of adults?* He started laughing and couldn't stop. Somehow the idea seemed even more hilarious in the light of day. When he got his hysterics under control, he made his way to the bathroom and started the shower, keeping the water colder than usual so he wouldn't fall back asleep.

Once clean, he dressed, downed a cup of coffee, and called Cal.

"Hey, Pax, what's up?"

"How busy are you in the late afternoon?"

"I've got a riding lesson that ends at four, and there'll be some chores to do after that, but I'm not crazy-busy. Why?"

"I was wondering if you could give Brad a tour of the farm then, or I could if you're too busy?"

"I bet you could."

Pax frowned at the phone. "What does that mean?"

"If you and Brad want a romantic stroll around the farm, why don't you just ask for it?"

"I didn't—"

Cal laughed. "I'd be happy to show Brad around. I'm assuming you'll be accompanying him, or are you just his travel service while he's here?"

"Fuck off." Pax had enjoyed pushing Cal and Beck toward each other. He was not enjoying being the one who was pushed.

"Brad came by the farm stand yesterday."

"Yeah, he mentioned that."

"Did he mention how he blushed when Beck said he should take you as his date to the reunion prom?"

Pax poured coffee into a huge travel mug. He was going to need gallons to get through the day. "No, but he did ask me."

"And you said yes?"

Pax could hear the laughter in his voice. "I did, and I know everyone will find out when we show up together, but if you wouldn't mind not saying anything…"

"Brad hasn't told his friends yet, has he?"

"That he's gay? No. He was going to when he went out with some of them last night, but Troy—"

"Troy is trouble."

"That's why he didn't say anything. They took him to the Get Down."

Cal sighed. "Yeah. Probably best not to mention it there."

They were both silent for a moment, then Cal said, "Are you okay, really? I'm no good with mushy shit, but…"

"Honestly? I don't know, but thanks for asking."

"All right. Beck and I are here if you need anything, okay?"

"Okay, and I'll see you later."

"Good. I'll show off my horses and the other animals, and then you can show Brad the gardens and the trail. No one will be out here then, so it will be *very private*."

"Are you suggesting I use your farm as a make-out spot?"

"I'm not suggesting anything."

Pax snorted. "Right."

"I gotta go. Beck's made me breakfast: cinnamon rolls, sausage, eggs—"

"Quit bragging."

"Play it right, and you might have a man to serve you too."

Pax heard a *thwack*.

"Hey!" Cal yelled.

"Sounds like Beck doesn't see things your way."

"He'd better if he knows what's good for him."

Pax rolled his eyes. "You're awful."

"I warned him of that, but he kept ignoring me."

"Go. I'll see you around four."

"See you then."

***

Pax never fully woke up that morning. He shuffled from one task to the next, not giving anything the attention it deserved. Cindy graciously agreed to give Irene and Elsie their lesson so he could rotate some of the items in the gallery and finish a painting of his own. He was thankful to be spared the questions they no doubt had about his date with Brad the day before.

When Cindy came into the studio around lunchtime, she studied him with narrowed eyes.

"What?" he asked, pushing his hair back with his hand and then wondering if he'd smeared paint on his face.

"You slept with him, didn't you?"

"No! Why would you say that?"

She smiled. "You've got that dazed, I've-been-fucked-all-night look."

"Cindy!"

She raised her brows. "Don't you 'Cindy' me; you know you do."

"Brad called me last night. We talked until late, and I didn't get much sleep."

She scowled at him. "You don't have to lie to me. I'm not going to tell anyone or pressure you for details."

He usually liked how perceptive Cindy was and how much she obviously cared, but he wished she would tone it down while Brad was in town.

"I'm not lying." *Just omitting some details.* "He did ask me to the prom, though."

Her eyes widened. "He what?"

Pax laughed, loving that he'd caught her off guard. "A group of obviously insane people decided to recreate their prom for the reunion."

Cindy grimaced. "That's a little much, isn't it?"

"It's worse than that. The theme is Cowboy Hoedown."

She almost dropped the files she was holding. "Okay, that's a lot too much."

He laughed. "Yeah, it is, but I have my cowboy outfit from the Jenkins Memorial fundraiser, so…"

As if the reality of what he'd said had finally hit her, she grinned. "You're going to the prom with Brad. That is so adorable. And I told you he was gay."

Pax couldn't help but smile at the way she'd gone from eye rolling to bouncing with excitement in seconds. "You did."

"I'm so happy for you."

"I thought you said the whole prom thing was too much."

Cindy glared at him. "Adults having a cowboy prom is ridiculous. You and Brad are adorable. Did you want him to take you to prom in high school?"

Pax shook his head. "I wanted to go out with Brad." *Okay, really, I just wanted to have sex with him. I was a teenage boy, for God's sake.* "But dances were on my list of stupid things only popular people were into."

"But you're going for Brad's sake."

"Yeah, for him I'll endure school dance hell in a cowboy costume."

She raised her brow. "I thought gay guys were supposed to be into cowboys."

Pax attempted a death glare, but laughter spilled over too quickly.

"I'm kidding," she said, though she was laughing almost too hard to talk. "Kind of."

He flipped her off. "Haven't I explained that

'gays' cannot be lumped into a single unit?"

She waved away his interjection. "I know. I know. But seriously, the cowboy thing?"

He sighed. "A hot, sculpted cowboy bare-chested on his mighty stallion. Yeah, I'm into that. But a bunch of high-school kids—or worse, adults acting like high-school kids—pretending to be cowboys? Not so exciting."

Cindy snorted. "Horrifying, most likely. But Brad in some assless chaps. That would be a fine sight."

If Pax had been drinking anything, he'd have spewed it across the room. As it was, he was simply rendered speechless for several seconds. "I can't believe you said that."

She winked at him. "Your man is seriously hot. What are you doing hanging around here? Don't you need to go get your hair done or have a pedicure or something to get yourself ready for your big night?"

"It's not until Saturday," Pax said, pushing his hair back again. "Do you think I need a haircut? Cal's going to give Brad a tour of his farm this afternoon, and I'm going too."

She grinned. "I was kidding about your hair, but a nice hot shower to get the paint off you and a relaxing soak in the tub would do you good. You've been stressed out for weeks. Go on. I'll watch the shop."

Maybe he'd been a little anxious about Brad being in town. Okay, a lot anxious. He'd hoped it hadn't showed, but of course Cindy noticed.

"I just might take you up on that." And he

might see if Max could fit him in for a haircut last-minute. It was getting a little long in front.

"Good. And I love the bright blue you've added."

Pax considered the canvas in front of him. He rather liked it too.

"Thanks."

She started to walk away and then turned. "Do you want me to come over on prom night and help you get ready?"

He glared at her.

"Aren't you supposed to have a bevy of friends over to get dressed with?"

Pax scowled. "Cindy, there are limits to our friendship."

She put a hand on his arm, and her expression turned serious. "I care about you, and I want everything with Brad to be perfect."

"I know, but I don't want to get my hopes up too much."

"I saw how that man looked at you. And that was before you agreed to be his prom date. Oooh, do you think he'll get you a corsage?"

Pax growled. "Cindy."

"Fine. I'm going to get back to work now." Just as she reached the door of the studio, she turned around once more. "I could do your nails."

"Out!"

Her cackles echoed in the studio as she walked briskly away.

Pax waited until she was back in the gallery to stop fighting his own laughter. What the fuck was he doing? He was thirty-four years old, and he was going to a reunion cowboy prom with the man he'd been fantasizing about for twenty years. That was going to be one fucked-up night.

He should be thrilled he was finally getting his fantasy—a date with Brad, multiple dates with Brad. Did a farm tour count as a date? Cal certainly seemed to think so. But what happened at the end of the week when Brad went back to Chicago?

Don't think that far ahead.

That was the sort of advice Pax always hated. He was a planner, he always had been, but this whole thing with Brad had never been in his plans, only his fantasies. Fantasies weren't actually supposed to come true.

You own a successful art gallery where you show some of your own work. Isn't that a fantasy come to life?

Day to day it didn't feel like it, but he supposed it was.

Maybe he did have a real chance with Brad, but thinking like that felt dangerous.

Most things worthwhile are.

Ugh. Now he was thinking in motivational posters.

He glanced at the time. He needed lunch; maybe that was why he couldn't seem to think clearly.

Chapter Eleven

Brad pulled up in front of the house where Bill and Janet Marsdon had lived when he was growing up. They'd moved several years before, but they'd kept the house as a rental. Now they wanted to sell. His parents had contacted him, knowing he was considering investing in properties to run as Airbnbs. They thought the house might be perfect since it was in walking distance of downtown, and there was a growing demand for places to stay in the area. Brad had initially intended to check out the house for that purpose. But after seeing Pax again, after realizing…

No, that was crazy.

Or was it?

It wasn't like he would have to move back permanently. He could have guests in the house when he didn't want to use it. He wanted to see Pax as frequently as he could. Why not stay in his own place instead of a motel?

Brenda, the real estate agent he was meeting, waited on the porch. She waved as he got out of his SUV. He glanced around, looking for signs of neglect, but from what he could see, the Marsdons had kept up with exterior maintenance. The paint looked new—they'd probably had it redone when they put it on the market—but he was glad they'd kept the same light-green color and the brick-red shutters. That combination really suited it.

"Do you want to start inside?" Brenda asked.

"I do. I haven't been inside in years. I know the Marsdons renovated the kitchen, and I'm excited to see what else has changed."

He hadn't been able to tell much from the pictures they'd included with the online listing, since they were taken at odd angles to show certain things to advantage.

He smiled as soon as he walked in. He'd always loved the high ceilings, the spacious foyer, and the living room with its beautiful bay window.

"You may know this since you're familiar with the house, but it was built in 1922, and these are the original hardwood floors."

Brad nodded. "That's good to know." He wasn't going to play up his interest too much, even knowing the Marsdons would give him a good price, but he was thrilled that they'd kept the floors as they were.

Brenda showed him the newly done kitchen, which was impressive but not too modern to fit the style of the house. They checked out the dining room, the bedrooms upstairs, the three baths, and the screened-in back porch. The bathrooms could use some renovating, but all-in-all it looked like it was in great shape.

Once he'd seen the interior, they toured the yard, including the large garden that some of the neighbors were tending.

"So what do you think?" Brenda asked.

"I need some time to consider it, but I'm feeling fairly good about it."

"All right. Just so you know, I do have

another interested party. I wouldn't want you to miss out on it."

"I'll give you a call later today or tomorrow."

"Excellent." She held out her hand, and they shook. As Brad turned to walk to his car, someone called him.

He looked at the house next door and saw Miss Elsie waving from her porch.

"Good morning," he called.

"Brad Watson. Irene told me you were in town. Are you looking at that house for your parents? We'd love to have them back."

Brad joined her on the porch so he wouldn't have to share his news with the entire neighborhood.

"I'll tell them you said so, but no, they're happy in Richmond. I was looking at the house for myself."

Her eyes sparkled. "So you're moving back?"

"Actually, I'm thinking of using it as a rental for tourists."

Elsie pursed her lips. "I don't know about that. Different people in and out all the time."

"Think of all the antics you could watch. You'd know all the tourist gossip."

She narrowed her eyes at him, and then the corner of her mouth quirked up. Soon she was slapping her leg and laughing. "You do know me, don't you."

"I do. And I'd be willing to keep the garden open to the neighborhood."

"That's good, but you ought to think about keeping it for yourself. I bet Paxton would enjoy having you around. He might even want to share the house, if it felt too big for you."

Brad sputtered. "Um… I don't think—"

She waved away his comment. "Don't you act like you don't know what I'm talking about. I heard you two already had lunch together."

"As friends."

She nodded. "You have to start somewhere."

He studied her for a moment. "What makes you think I like men?"

She brushed that comment off as well. "You like Pax. That I can see. As to who else you might date, that's none of my business."

That was an interestingly progressive take on things. "I'll keep your suggestion in mind."

"You two would be the best neighbors."

The best source of gossip.

"Aaand. You could be taste testers for my cakes and pies."

"Now that is tempting."

She grinned. "Do think about Pax. I know I'm being an interfering busybody, but he deserves some happiness."

"I do think about him, Miss Elsie. I think about him a lot."

"Good."

As she pulled him into a tight hug, he realized he'd forgotten just how much he loved some of Ames Bridge's more colorful citizens.

***

A little after four, Brad texted Pax, saying he was in the lot behind Pax's building. Pax had offered to meet him at the farm, but Brad wanted to pick him up.

When Pax stepped out of the building, Brad's mouth dropped open. Holy fuck. Pax had gotten his hair cut, and damn, Brad needed the name of his stylist. He was wearing jeans that hugged his legs and a chocolate-brown-and-tan-striped shirt that was perfect for his eyes and skin. Brad wanted to skip the farm tour and take Pax right back to his room to do what he'd lain awake fantasizing about for hours. Alcohol knocked most people out, but he never slept well after drinking.

He cleared his throat as Pax got into the car. *Act civilized.* "How was your day?"

"Fine. It wasn't easy to stay awake, though. How about you?"

Heat crept into Brad's face. "Sorry. I know that's my fault. If it's any consolation, let's just say my day started off rough."

Pax laughed. "I could've guessed."

"I recovered, though, and I visited Irene." He wasn't ready to tell Pax about seeing Elsie while he checked out the Marsdons' house.

"How was she?"

"Stubborn, talkative, bossy."

"So like usual," Pax said.

"Yes, delightfully so. I told her I'm gay."

"You did?" Brad could hear his surprise.

"Yep. She—"

Pax gestured toward the road. "You turn the other way to go to the farm."

Brad laid a hand on Pax's thigh. Whoa. There was that zing again. Pax gasped and tried to cover it with a cough.

"I know, but I wanted to talk to you first. I

texted Cal and told him we'd be a few minutes late. "
Too high-handed? Probably, but he wanted some time
alone.

"Where are we going?"

"Just to the bridge, like we did the other day."

"Okay." Pax didn't say anything else, but
Brad could feel his tension. Maybe he was assuming
too much.

Brad pulled into the parking lot by the bridge.
He opened his door, and Pax followed suit. "Over
there?" Brad asked, pointing to the most secluded
table.

"Sure."

Brad sat down next to Pax, both of them
facing the water.

"So Irene?" Pax asked, his voice a little shaky.
"How did she react?"

Was Pax as nervous as he was? "She said
she'd suspected it, and then when she saw us at
Trish's, she was sure."

"How did she know?"

Brad turned to face him, wanting to see his
reaction. "The way I looked at you. That's what she
said."

"Oh." Pax's gaze darted away. He sounded
more concerned than surprised.

"I didn't know I was giving myself away."

"You aren't; not to everybody, anyway."

"Troy and them haven't seen me with you."

Pax nodded. "But they will."

"Yeah, they will, but I have no intention of
hiding that you're my date. I wouldn't have asked you
to go with me if I did."

"And once they know…"

Brad shrugged. "They can think what they want. All I care about is that I'll be there with you."

"Brad, what are we—"

"You promised me a kiss today."

He deserves an answer to his question.

Brad ignored that irritating voice in his head.

Pax glanced at him and then turned back to the water. "I did?"

"Yes, last night."

"You remember that?"

"I do."

"Oh." Pax licked his lips, and Brad fought to be patient. He was already pushing Pax, probably harder than he should.

"I'm ready to claim it," he said after a few moments of Pax silently rubbing his foot in the grass.

"Here?"

Brad looked around. No one else was there at the moment, and they were hidden by the trees. "Yes, here."

Pax shifted, turning toward him. Brad cupped his face in one hand and leaned closer. "May I kiss you now?"

Pax nodded. His lips parted slightly.

Brad moved closer…closer… Then his lips were on Pax's, and it felt so right.

He started off gentle. A careful touch, his tongue tracing Pax's lower lip. Then Pax moaned and reached for him, pulling him closer.

"Open for me." Brad breathed the words into him.

Pax did, and Brad accepted the invitation. He

slid his tongue over Pax's and then flicked it over the roof of his mouth, needing to taste and feel all of him.

Pax pushed his hands into Brad's hair. "Need you," he whispered.

Brad needed him too, but they were in public. They needed to slow down. Reluctantly, Brad pulled away. "We can't do this here."

Pax nodded. "I know, but I…"

"Don't want to stop? Me either."

Pax's breathing was ragged, his eyes wide. Did they really need to see Cal's farm?

"That was even better than I thought it would be," Brad said.

"Y-yeah. It was."

He grinned and brushed his fingers over Pax's. "After the farm tour, we could pick up where we left off."

Pax groaned. "I have a painting event tonight."

"After that?"

"Um… Wait, don't you have the sports get-together thing?"

"Shit!" A few of the other athletes from his class had set up a dinner to relive their glory days. He'd been mildly looking forward to it since he'd get to see his former coaches. Now he wished he'd said he couldn't go.

"How late will that last?"

"I have no idea."

Pax laughed. "Well, there's always prom night."

"I can't wait that long."

Brad leaned down again until only inches

separated them. He breathed deeply. He was sure the citrusy scent of Pax's soap would now make him hard anytime he smelled it. "I want you, Paxton Marshall. I want to strip you naked, lay you out on my bed, and explore every inch of you."

"Oh… You do?"

"I do."

The sound of a car coming up the road to the bridge startled them both, and they jumped apart.

"I guess we should see Cal's farm now," Brad said.

Pax nodded. "But I… I want that. What you just said."

Brad grinned. "And you'll get it as soon as we have more time."

"Go!" Pax motioned toward the car.

Brad did, because otherwise he was in danger of forgetting why it mattered if someone saw him take Pax right there on the bench.

They didn't talk any more as Brad drove them to Cal's farm. It was all Brad could do to concentrate on driving with most of his blood swelling his dick.

When he pulled into Cal's driveway, he glanced at Pax.

"You okay?" Brad asked.

"I'm… Yeah."

Brad chuckled. "If you get that worked up over a kiss, I can't wait to see what happens when we actually have some privacy."

"*Braaad.*"

"What?"

"We have to see Cal and Beck in a few seconds."

Brad waved a hand dismissively. "They already know I want you."

"They'll be teasing me forever. You don't have to live here."

"Not for now anyway," Brad said.

Pax's frown told him he shouldn't have said that. "What does that mean?"

"As a consultant I could live anywhere. We'll talk about it later."

"You don't want to live in Ames Bridge."

Brad ignored that and opened his car door. "Later."

Chapter Twelve

Brad waved when Cal and Beck came out of the barn. Hopefully, if he distracted them with enough questions, they wouldn't notice he was still half-hard from teasing Pax mercilessly.

"Welcome to the farm," Cal called.

"It's impressive. I can't believe how different it looks from when I used to come out and pick up eggs or jam for my mom."

"He's worked so hard on it." The wistful look on Beck's face made Brad pause. Did he look at Pax like that? If so, it was no wonder Irene knew he was gay.

"Come on." Cal motioned. "Let me show you how I remodeled the barn, and you can meet some of the horses."

Beck grinned. "You're getting the behind-the-scenes personal tour."

Pax sniffed. "I should hope so."

"Pax and Cal worked together on a fundraiser a few months ago," Beck said. "They're cooking up some more plans for a creativity day. Hopefully they can even draw in some tourists too."

"We're going to do it when the leaves are at their peak," Pax added.

They were in the foothills, so the leaves weren't as incredible as they were in the mountains, but they still gave a nice show. Fall was a good time to draw tourists.

"That sounds great!"

Cal nodded. "What Beck isn't saying is that he's the one coordinating it."

"He's keeping me busy with events as well as helping at the farm."

"You do more than help, baby."

Beck grinned.

Cal seemed so relaxed and happy, Brad couldn't help himself. "This is kind of a personal question, but I heard you had some rough times when you two first got together."

Cal smiled, and Beck laid a hand on his shoulder. "Yeah, it sucked at first when people found out."

Brad shifted his gaze to Pax, but Pax was studying the ground.

"The fact that they found out when Mrs. Johnson caught us naked in the barn didn't help," Beck added.

"Shit! Her husband's a deacon at the Tabernacle, right?" Brad asked.

Cal snorted. "He is, the bigoted bastard."

"But you're doing okay now?"

"Yeah, once I decided Beck was more important than anything else, we've been making it work."

Wow. Cal really had changed. That might be the most romantic thing Brad had ever heard anyone say. He wanted the kind of happiness they had. This time when he looked at Pax, their gazes met, and Pax nervously licked his lips.

"The farm's doing better than ever." Beck's

words startled him back to reality.

"This summer we've seen more tourists than any summer yet," Cal said. "And I've got two fall weddings scheduled to happen in the new flower gardens."

"That was my idea," Beck chimed in. Cal swatted his ass.

Brad laughed. "That's fantastic."

"So there're some loud assholes who'd like to run the two of us—and probably Pax too—out of town. But I love this farm, and they aren't making us leave."

"And there are far more people who will support you," Beck added.

"It wasn't easy starting the gallery here, but I've done it, and at this point it's rare that anyone complains where I can hear it."

Beck nodded. "And you're not just running a gallery and painting shop. "You're creating an arts community. I wouldn't have thought that was possible before I came back here."

"Came back and stayed," Brad observed.

Beck grinned. "Yeah. Someone made Ames Bridge more tempting than I thought possible."

Brad glanced over at Pax, who seemed to be studiously not meeting his eyes. "I can understand that."

What would Pax think about the idea of Brad moving back to Ames Bridge? He wanted to know, but he'd have to be patient. And yet he'd waited twenty years already. How much more patience could he have?

He wanted more from Pax, and when he

wanted something, he went for it. And after their kiss, Brad knew for certain that Pax was The One. He'd dated men he cared for, and he'd enjoyed the hell out of plenty of recreational fucking, but he'd never felt like this about anyone. If his desire for Pax had lasted for decades, it had to be serious. He just had to make Pax see that too.

"I'm going to go get some paperwork done in the office." Beck's words interrupted Brad's thoughts. "But I'm sure I'll see you before you leave."

"Sure. We'll say bye. It's been great to see you again. I guess you were probably twelve the last time I saw you."

"Probably so." Beck winced. "I was a mess back then."

Cal snorted. "You're not much better at twenty-eight."

Beck stuck his tongue out.

Brad loved the interplay between those two. "I doubt I was any better back in those days."

"You weren't," Pax teased.

"You hush, or I'll talk about your high-school years." Brad barely resisted the urge to spank him like Cal had done to Beck.

Color rose in Pax's face. "Let's all hush up about the past."

"Good idea," Cal said. "Follow me."

They walked into the barn. It was clean and light and not at all what Brad expected.

Cal waved him farther in. "Come meet our newest addition. This is Ragweed, he's two months old, and this"—he pointed to the next stall—"is his mother, Fern."

The foal was adorable. Brad and Pax fed him hay and watched him for several minutes before Cal showed them more horses and then took them to see the heritage breed pigs he was raising as well as his variety of free-ranging chickens.

They walked over a hill and came to the vegetable gardens and the orchard where the blackberry canes were thick with berries.

Cal gestured toward the abundance. "Feel free to pick some if you'd like."

Pax grabbed a fat berry and popped it into his mouth. It was so juicy that some dripped down his chin. Brad longed to lick it off. Instead he got a berry for himself and then another.

"These are fantastic. I gave one of the baskets I bought to Miss Irene and then wished I hadn't. I need to get more for myself."

Cal grinned. "I'm glad you like them. I've got some I picked earlier at the house. I'll send some with you."

"Thanks."

"What about me?" Pax glared at him.

"Get him to share." Cal inclined his head toward Brad.

"I'd be happy to."

"See?" Cal turned to Brad. "I've got some chores to do at the barn. Pax knows his way around, so he can show you the flower garden and the trail."

"A riding trail?"

"Yes, but you can walk it too."

"They're offering trail rides now," Pax said.

"Oh, I bet the tourists love that."

Cal nodded. "It's been going well so far. The

trail's all shady, so it's relatively cool even in this heat wave we've been having."

"Are you sure you don't mind us walking around for a while?" Brad asked.

"Not at all. I thought you might like a little privacy."

"That would be very nice." He looked at Pax, but Pax kept his eyes on Cal.

"Enjoy, then," Cal called as he headed toward the horse barn.

"So which way do we go?"

"Follow me."

Brad was happy to, since he got a perfect view of Pax's ass as they walked downhill.

"Remember how Beck's grandma used to sell flowers?" Pax asked.

"Oh yeah. Sometimes my mom would have me get some from her when she sent me to the McMurtrys for eggs."

"Well, Beck thought Cal should plant a flower garden both for decoration and to sell. They arranged them in a hexagon, and when the blooms are full, they're magnificent. See?"

Pax pointed to the left, and Brad followed the line of his arm.

"Wow! That looks great."

"The weddings will be there in the garden, with the bride and groom under the trellis."

"I can see why people want to get married here."

Pax nodded. "What Cal and Beck didn't say is that they'll also be getting married here."

"Really?"

"Yes. Apparently Cal proposed in a moment of desperation when he was trying to convince Beck to stay in Ames Bridge. To his shock, Beck said yes. They decided to wait until next spring, but when the first flowers are in bloom, they'll have their wedding right here."

Pax continued down the hill toward the garden, but Brad just stood there. *Married. What if...* No. It was way too soon. He was jumping in without thinking again. But it sounded like Cal had done the same thing, and look how well it worked out for him.

Brad looked down at the garden and imagined Pax standing under the trellis, which was covered in pink roses. In his mind, he stood next to Pax, holding his hand, promising to stay with him forever. He'd promise it right that minute if Pax wouldn't think he was crazy for doing so.

"Brad? You okay?" Pax had stopped and was watching him.

"Um...yeah. Yeah, I am."

He ran down the hill to catch up. Pax gave him a quizzical look, but he didn't say anything about him spacing out.

"The trail starts over there." He pointed to the sign indicating that both horse riders and pedestrians were welcome, but not bicycles. "Cal cleaned up the area around the entrance and made the trail wider than it used to be. It's perfect for group rides now."

"Shall we try it out?"

"For a walk?"

Brad grinned. "Or...other things."

Pax frowned. "Is that a good idea?"

"The best."

"It's not that private."

Brad looked around. They were completely alone. "Cal said no one else was out here this afternoon. He'd know, right?"

"We'll still be outside."

Brad shrugged.

"We could...um...look at all the types of flowers first."

Brad sighed. "You're impossible."

"No, I'm..."

What could Brad say to goad him without really insulting him? "Dignified? Sensible?"

"Ugh, you make me sound like a first-class prig."

"No prig kisses like you do."

"No, but... This is all..."

Brad nodded. "I know. It's taken us both by surprise." He reached out and took Pax's hand. "That doesn't mean it's wrong."

"No, it doesn't."

"So...a walk?"

"Okay," Pax agreed.

He kept hold of Pax's hand and laced their fingers together.

Pax was very quiet, and Brad began to feel like despite their physical connection, there was a partition between them.

"What are you thinking about?" he asked.

"What did you mean about not living here 'for now'?"

How much should he say? "Well, the Marsdons—you remember them? They were friends of my parents. Their daughter Ginny was—"

117

"A cheerleader. I remember. They moved away a few years ago."

"Right. They've been riding around in their RV. But now they're moving to Arizona, and they want to sell their house."

"They do?"

"Yes. They asked my parents if they knew of anyone who might be interested in it, and…well, I'm thinking about buying it."

"What?" Pax stumbled, nearly pulling them both down. "Why?"

"According to almost everyone I've talked to, Ames Bridge is an up-and-coming town. So I figure it's a great place to own a rental property or an Airbnb I could use occasionally."

"So you wouldn't live there?"

Brad wasn't sure if that was disappointment or relief in Pax's voice. Pax seemed to be working hard to keep his tone neutral. "Not all the time. I'd still need to spend some time in Chicago, at least for a while. And I travel a lot. But I could be there some of the time or maybe—"

"Brad, I meant what I said about you not wanting to live here."

"You don't want me here? You wouldn't want to—"

"What I don't want is for you to be unhappy."

Brad sighed. "What if being around you is what makes me happy?"

Pax ducked to avoid an overhanging branch. "You've been in town two days, and we haven't seen each other for more than a few hours at a time in twenty years."

"We spent plenty of time together during the summers when I was in college."

Pax rolled his eyes. "Okay, sixteen years, but the point is—"

"I still want you. And I think"—his pulse pounded, and he had to push the words past a lump in his throat—"I *hope* you feel the same way." What if he was wrong?

Pax sighed. "I do, but…"

"The distance is the main reason you're feeling reluctant about this, right?"

"The distance? Yeah, that's an important factor, but how you'll feel after you come out is a bigger one. The shit you'll get. Brad, this isn't Chicago."

"No, it's much warmer."

"Brad!"

He held up his hands. "Okay, no more joking. I know this all sounds crazy."

"Yeah, it kinda does."

"But we've wanted each other forever, and now we have a chance. I want to do whatever is necessary to make that work."

"Does an adolescent crush really make a good basis for a grown-up relationship?"

Brad shrugged. "I don't know, but we can't find out if we don't try."

"Just don't do something crazy until you see what it's like when we show up together Saturday night."

"Beck stayed despite the homophobic assholes here."

"But he and Cal—"

"Exactly. They had each other."

"But they'd been together for a while."

"Only a month or so from what I heard."

"Six weeks I think, but it's a hell of a lot more than two days."

Brad sighed. If he kept pushing, he'd just piss Pax off, and that was the opposite of what he wanted. Swallowing his hurt and annoyance, he said, "I want you to know it's a possibility, okay? I can do my job from anywhere. If I buy this house, I don't have to live in it. Depending on the contracts I secure for the next year, I might be able to keep my apartment in Chicago even if I don't rent it out. Then I could be flexible."

"Okay. I guess that makes sense. Kinda."

At least Pax didn't look horrified like he had a few moments ago. He still seemed wary, but Brad was no longer afraid he was going to run and not look back. Brad was being too impulsive once again. He was ready to dive right in with no safety precautions. He shouldn't blame Pax for wanting to be sure they weren't setting themselves up for disaster.

"We'll talk about it later, okay? After everyone knows about us, or about me, I guess I should say."

Pax stopped, and Brad turned to face him. "Us. This is about us, even if I'm...unsure, even if I can't imagine you being happy here. I still want you, and I'll be right there with you to face whatever shit comes of us going to 'prom' together."

"I... I'm glad."

***

They started walking again. After a few

moments of silence, Pax said, "The farm's impressive, isn't it?"

"It sure is. Cal's impressive too."

Pax was jealous for about half a second, but Cal was the kind of man everybody noticed. "Right? Those arms."

Brad laughed. "I actually meant the work he's done, but you're right. He's fucking hot."

That's what he got for making assumptions. He hoped his face wasn't as red as he feared. "Beck's a lucky man."

"Not as lucky as I'd be if a certain man let me continue what we started at the bridge earlier."

Pax wanted that, but the last thing they needed was to get caught like Cal and Beck had. "But anyone could—"

"No one else is out here," Brad insisted. "And look." He gestured toward a large oak just off the path. "A big sturdy tree perfectly made to support a man's back while he's being fucked within an inch of his life."

Pax sucked in his breath, and Brad turned to look at him. "You like when I talk dirty."

"I…uh…"

He grinned. "You do."

Pax nodded. He'd always loved that, but he'd never been with a man who did it so boldly when they weren't even in bed.

"So are we going to take advantage of what nature has so thoughtfully provided?"

"Um…"

Brad began walking toward the tree, tugging Pax along with him. Then he took hold of Pax's hips and spun them around so Pax's back was against the solid trunk.

Brad ran a finger along his jaw. "Tell me what you want."

Pax opened his mouth, but no words came out. Brad's low, sexy voice had scrambled his senses.

"I like that I've rendered you speechless, but I want to be absolutely sure you like what's happening here."

Pax licked his lips and swallowed as he tried to remember how to talk. "I…"

"Yes?"

"Kiss me."

"As you wish." Brad took hold of Pax's hands, pulled them above his head, and pinned them to the tree, gently enough that the bark didn't scratch him.

"Do you like being held down?"

"I…" Pax looked everywhere but at Brad.

"Tell me."

"Yes, I…" Pax squirmed, tilting his hips so he could grind against Brad. "Like it."

"Mmm." Brad thrust against him, giving him the friction he needed. "Ah, yes. I think you do."

Pax nodded frantically. "I like…men who…take charge."

"Good. I'm going to kiss you now, and you're not going to move, you understand?"

"I…"

Brad shook his head. "Don't talk either."

Pax bit back a whimper. Brad was fucking amazing.

Pax held himself rigid, practically vibrating

with tension. But he kept his hips still, and he didn't fight Brad's hold. Brad kissed him softly, licking, teasing, sucking on his lower lip, tracing the line of the top one before pushing in, letting his tongue tangle with Pax's. Pax gave in to the urge to kiss him back then but resisted the urge to lift his hips, despite being ready to beg for friction. The kiss grew more and more intense until he and Brad seemed to be doing battle. Still he held the rest of his body tight and rigid.

Just as Pax was growing desperate for air, Brad pulled back.

Pax stared at him, panting. "That was…"

"Yeah, it was." He let go of Pax's wrists. "Arms at your sides."

Pax did as he said, his gaze never leaving Brad's.

"Perfect."

Brad ran a hand over Pax's chest. When he flicked a blunt nail over Pax's nipple through his shirt, he shuddered and pressed hard against the tree, fighting his need to move.

"Oh yeah. That's very good."

Brad's hand moved lower until he brushed it over Pax's cock. *Fuck.* Much more of that and he'd be hard enough to burst right through the zipper.

Pax scrabbled at the bark, digging his fingers in as Brad rubbed the heel of his hand up and down Pax's erection.

"Fuck, Brad. I need to move. Need to touch you."

Brad dropped his hand and stepped closer, fitting their bodies together. He tugged on one of

Pax's thighs, encouraging him to lift his leg and wrap it around Brad.

"Please," Pax begged, no longer caring if he sounded desperate.

"Wrap your arms around my neck."

Pax did, and Brad took hold of his ass and lifted him.

"Lean back; I've got you," Brad said as Pax wrapped his legs around Brad's waist.

Pax realized he trusted Brad completely. "You've always protected me."

"I want to protect you from the things people will say when they find out we're...whatever we are."

"Dating?" Pax asked. Were they?

Brad nodded and then kissed Pax again. Pax couldn't stay still anymore; he ground his hips against Brad, and Brad thrust back, pushing him into the tree. Pax groaned, tongue sliding along Brad's as Brad worked his hips, faster and harder. Pax tried to meet each thrust, but their position didn't make that easy.

"Let me do the work," Brad said.

"Can't keep still."

Brad laughed against the warm skin of his neck and then kissed his way down to Pax's collarbone. He used tongue and teeth to tease the sensitive flesh there.

"More," Pax begged.

They were both making desperate sounds by the time Brad turned his attention back to Pax's mouth.

"Need more," Pax whispered between kisses.

"Me too."

Brad reached between them and worked the

fastening of Pax's jeans. Pax tried to help him, but he started to slip, so he tightened his legs and held Brad's shoulder with one hand.

"I've got you." Brad squeezed his ass as if to demonstrate. "All that time I've been putting in at the gym is paying off. I couldn't have done this a few years ago."

Pax laughed. "I'm impressed."

"Good."

When they finally succeeded in freeing their cocks, Brad took them both in his hand and stroked. Pax watched as his hand moved up and down. When Brad eased his palm over their heads, Pax gasped.

"Like that?"

"I like all of this."

"Mmm." Brad worked them slowly. Even so, Pax was rushing toward climax at an alarming speed. He fought to hold back, because he didn't want this to end.

Pax's ass began to vibrate, and he wondered for a second how the hell Brad was doing that. Then he realized it was his phone.

"Ignore it," Brad whispered, but Pax was already trying to reach for it.

"It could be Cindy," he said. "She's alone at the gallery."

Brad groaned, but he lowered Pax to the ground and stepped back.

"It's Cal." Pax answered the call.

"Sorry to bother you, but one of my boarders just showed up, and she's going to ride the trail. I wanted to give you a heads-up so you could watch out for her. She'd probably freak if she found you two naked."

"W-we're not. We weren't—"

"With a man like that after you, why the hell not?"

"Cal!"

His laugh echoed in Pax's ear as he ended the call.

"What's wrong?" Brad asked.

"One of the people who board their horses here is headed this way. He was calling to warn us."

"Because he thought we were doing exactly what we were?"

"Yeah." Heat rose in Pax's face.

"I love how easily you get embarrassed."

Pax scowled at him as they straightened their clothes. "I just don't like admitting we were acting like a couple of teenagers."

"You think Beck and Cal don't? I'd take advantage of every inch of this place if I lived here."

"You would?"

"Sure. Sex in the barn, sex in the woods. Okay, maybe the chicken yard should be off-limits."

Pax laughed. "I'm sure there's someone out there with a kink that would fulfill, but it's not for me."

"I'm glad to hear that."

They started walking briskly down the trail. "Please tell me we have time to finish this, because I might die otherwise."

Pax raised his brows.

"Fine. I would likely survive, but it won't be comfortable."

Pax wasn't comfortable himself. His dick was

protesting the hell out of being stuffed back in his jeans. "I warned you that I had a gathering at the shop tonight, and you've got the sports thing. It's already—" He pulled his phone out. "It's six."

"Shit, my thing's at seven."

"Mine too. See? No time."

Brad sighed. "I guess it's really for the best. When I finally have you, I want to take my time."

His words made Pax shiver, and they did nothing good for the state of his dick.

"How early will you be up tomorrow?" Brad asked.

"Are you serious?" No way was he fucking Brad for the first time before work. He wouldn't be able to focus on anything.

"I'm dying here, Pax."

"Not early enough."

"Okay, but I don't care if it has to happen on the street downtown, at a booth in Trish's, or on the high-school lawn. I will fuck you tomorrow night."

Pax almost grabbed him and pushed him up against a tree and to hell with the woman who could come riding by any minute. "Now *you're* the one killing *me*."

"Good. We should both suffer."

They laughed, and Brad took his hand. Pax was restless and horny and he hated like hell that they had been interrupted. But he was also enjoying just being with Brad, laughing, talking, touching with no agenda. Maybe this could work out after all.

Chapter Thirteen

Around ten that night, Pax had finally gotten the painting space cleaned up, showered the paint off himself, and curled up in bed with a cup of tea and his e-reader. He'd read maybe five pages when his phone rang.

Please be something I can ignore.

It was Brad.

Hoping he wasn't drunk and needing a ride again, Pax answered. "Hello."

"What are you doing?"

His low voice made the simplest phrases sound lascivious. "I'm in bed, reading. Aren't you at the sports dinner?"

"No. It was just as boring as the ones in high school, so I left early. Do you want to come over here? I'd come to you, since you're already in bed, but I don't think I should drive."

"You didn't do shots again, did you?"

"No!"

Pax laughed.

"I just downed enough wine to drown out the boring speeches."

"Understandable. How'd you get home?"

"You remember Stephanie Miller? She basically single-handedly helped our girls basketball team win the state championship."

"Right. Did you know she's a plumber now

and she's dating Roscoe?"

"The plumber part I knew, but not the other. Really?"

"Yeah, she married that shithead she was with in high school. He just sat around smoking and never did anything, so she finally left him, went to school, got certified as a plumber, and now she and Roscoe seem really happy."

"That's great. She sat next to me and was as bored as I was, so she took me home."

"At least you had someone to talk to."

"I'd have tried to leave even earlier if it weren't for her. You want to come over and finish what we started in the woods?"

No way in hell would his cock let him say no, even if part of him really wanted a good night's sleep. "I do."

"Thank God! How fast can you be here?"

Pax laughed. "You're so impatient."

"And you're not? You were begging for it earlier."

Pax was sure his face was rapidly turning red. Thank goodness Brad couldn't see him. "I'll be there in fifteen minutes."

"Make it ten."

"If I get a speeding ticket, it will just take longer."

Brad sighed. "Just hurry."

Pax laughed as he ended the call.

***

Pax pulled into the lot at the Bridge Motel. His car was rather distinct, an aging blue Prius, not a hell of a lot of those in town, except ones driven by tourists. With luck, anyone passing by would think that's exactly what it was—a tourist's car. If anyone recognized it as his, he and Brad would be the talk of the town the next day. No one was going to believe he and Brad were just reminiscing about old times. Sooner or later everyone would know anyway, but he wanted Brad to be able to come out on his own terms.

He'd encouraged Cal and Beck, and he wasn't sorry for that. But now that he thought about living through what they had, the reactions people would have, the way they'd bring up Rob and what he would've thought—and he had no doubt some people would—he wondered if he had the strength to deal with it.

He stepped from his car and shut the door. It sounded extra loud, but he didn't care. He walked quickly toward Brad's room, hoping no one would see him. As he lifted his hand to knock, everything felt surreal. After all this time, Brad was going to fuck him, and based on what happened earlier, Brad was everything Pax could want in a bed partner.

Could this be real? He pinched himself just for good measure.

Ow! Well, he wasn't dreaming.

Brad opened the door so fast, Pax wondered if he'd been standing right behind it.

He pulled Pax in and pushed the door closed, turned the lock, and gave Pax a slow once-over. "Strip."

Pax's cock swelled. "And if I don't want to obey?"

"You do."

He did. No point in pretending otherwise.

"You're very sure of yourself."

"When it comes to this—between us—yes, I am."

Pax swallowed a sigh. "Do you know how fucking sexy that is?"

He grinned. "Yes. Now don't make me ask again."

"Were you asking?"

Brad's eyes widened for just a fraction of a second. Then he gave Pax an arrogant leer. "No, I wasn't."

"Good."

Pax yanked his T-shirt over his head and tossed it to the floor. He froze in the midst of unbuttoning his shorts. The way Brad was looking at him made him feel like a rabbit about to be devoured by a wolf.

"Keep going," Brad ordered.

Pax kicked out of his shoes, then undid his shorts and pushed them and his briefs to the floor. After he stepped out of them, he wrapped a hand around his cock, which was already fully hard. He stroked it slowly, meeting Brad's gaze.

"Fuck, you're hot." Brad looked even hungrier than before.

Pax smiled, trying not to feel self-conscious standing there with Brad still fully dressed.

Brad moved closer. Then he shocked Pax by dropping to his knees. Pax swayed with dizziness when Brad swiped his tongue over the tip of Pax's cock. He thought he might fall over, but Brad gripped his hips to steady him. Then he glanced up, a wicked grin on his face.

"Um…" Pax wasn't sure what he intended to say. Did he mean to beg Brad to continue? He sure as hell wasn't going to tell him to stop. He lost the last of his ability to think when Brad swallowed him down, inch by inch, seeming to savor his cock. He worked his tongue along the underside, and Pax shuddered. It was all he could do not to thrust into Brad's mouth.

When Brad had taken him almost all the way, he pulled back. Pax bit his lip, wanting to protest the loss of that soft heat. Brad teased him, dipping into the slit, flicking his tongue over the head, and then finally taking him down again and setting a steady rhythm as he sucked, lips sliding along Pax's length.

Heat built in his balls. Brad's mouth felt so damn good. He needed. He… "Brad, I…"

Brad looked up at him and smiled around his cock.

Pax shook his head. "Can't last."

Brad pulled off long enough to say "Then don't."

Pax made shallow thrusts, unable to help himself. Brad didn't pull back or hesitate; he kept working Pax with tongue, lips, and just enough teeth to suggest pain but never give it. Then he cupped Pax's balls. At first he simply weighed them in his hand, his touch light, teasing. Then his grip grew firmer as he tugged with one hand while working the fingers of his other along Pax's crack.

All it took was pressure against his hole, and Pax was done for. He thrust deeper than he meant to as climax took him by surprise. His hands flexed on Brad's scalp as Brad pressed a finger inside him, teasing his ass as he sucked Pax until it was too much and Pax pushed at his shoulders.

Brad let go of him and sat back.

Pax lowered himself to the floor. No way could he stay on his feet after what might have been the best orgasm of his life.

Brad raised his brows. "I can fuck you on the floor, but I think the bed's a better idea."

Pax gave a half-hearted laugh. "Give me a minute. You can't expect me to move after that, can you?"

"I'm going to have to build up your stamina."

"Maybe you need to stop being so devastating."

"Really?"

"No."

Brad laughed as he stood and began to shuck his clothes. Pax stayed right where he was and watched. Brad's pecs and his well-defined abs were a sight worth appreciating. "Wow."

Brad smiled. "Like what you see?"

"I...yeah. You were fit in high school, but now... Fuck, you look amazing."

"Thanks."

Brad shoved his athletic shorts and briefs down, and his cock sprang up, hard, thick, and just as big as it had looked through his tiny shorts.

"That's impressive."

Brad grinned. "Wait until you see what I can do with it."

Considering what he could do with his mouth, Pax wasn't sure he'd survive it. He forced himself to his feet. He wanted Brad inside him, wanted to feel possessed by him. But fear was also part of what was making his heart pound. Pax had created a safe world for himself. Sure, sometimes it was a lonely world, but it was safe. Whether Brad stayed for a while or went right back to Chicago, he was going to shake things up. He already had, but once Pax opened to him like this, once Brad had been as close to him—inside him—as he could be, Pax didn't know how anything would ever feel the same.

He lay down on the bed, and Brad grabbed a condom and lube from the shaving kit sitting on the nightstand. Pax dropped his legs open as Brad settled between them and let his gaze roam up and down Pax's body.

Pax fought the urge to squirm under the intense scrutiny. He'd kept in shape, but he wasn't ripped like Brad.

Brad caught his gaze then. Pax wasn't sure how to read the look on his face. "What?"

"It's really you. Here. With me."

Pax nodded. "Yeah."

"I don't know where to start."

"What you just did was good."

Brad chuckled. "I'm glad you enjoyed it. Would you touch yourself and let me watch?"

"Aren't you…? I mean, haven't you waited long enough?" Surely his cock was aching after what they'd already done.

With an arrogant arch of his brow, Brad said, "I can hold out as long as I need to."

Pax rolled his eyes, but he took his cock in hand and started stroking.

His cock slowly came back to life. He

increased the speed of his strokes, growing more and more desperate for friction.

"That's it. Let me see how good it feels, how much you want my cock in you, stretching your ass, owning you."

Holy fuck, that was hot! Pax arched off the bed. "Yes, need you."

***

Brad slicked up a finger and teased Pax's hole. When he pushed inside, Pax winced.

"Damn, you're tight."

"Yeah."

Brad worked deeper, and Pax kept stroking himself.

"Hands over your head. It's my turn now."

Pax groaned as he obeyed. Damn, Brad loved how he responded to commands. He worked Pax's cock as he pushed deeper. But when he added a second finger, Pax tensed again.

"Sorry, it's…been a while. More than a while, really."

"Like how long?"

"Um…a year or…more."

"Why?" Brad winced. He shouldn't have said that. "I just mean that you're so gorgeous and… I can't imagine anyone not wanting you."

"Everyone knows everyone here. If you load up Grindr here, you'll learn things you might wish you didn't know."

Brad snorted. "I bet. But Greensboro? Charlotte?"

Pax sighed. "The gallery kind of became my life, and then… I don't know. I've been out to clubs a few times, messed around with a few guys, but there wasn't anyone I wanted to do this with. It hasn't been worth the effort for ages, not until…"

"Until?"

"You came back." He frowned. "That sounds so…"

Brad shook his head. "No, it doesn't. I'll go slow, okay?"

"I'll be all right. You don't have to—"

"You're going to enjoy this." No way was he doing anything that hurt Pax.

"I will once I—"

"All of this."

He pressed two fingers in again, but so slowly he was barely moving. By the time he'd gone as deep as he could, he felt sure Pax was panting more from need than from the stretch.

Then he curled his digits forward, and Pax's hips shot off the bed.

Ah, yes, just the right spot. "Good, isn't it?"

"Brad, I—"

He did it again.

Pax cried out and pushed against him, trying to take his fingers deeper.

"More?" Brad asked.

"Yes! Please!"

He eased out, and then cautious of giving Pax too much pressure, he added another finger.

"Okay?" Brad asked.

Pax nodded. Brad pushed in just a tiny bit farther and twisted his hand. Pax writhed, working his hips, trying to take more. He was so damn hot. Why had they waited this long?

"Ready for more?" Brad asked, pitching his voice low.

Pax opened his eyes and looked up. After a few ragged breaths, he said, "I've been ready."

"Really?"

Pax licked his lips. "Yes."

"Good. Turn over. I want you on your hands and knees."

Pax's eyes widened. Then he quickly positioned himself.

"Perfect." Brad slid a few slick fingers down his crack and teased the edge of his hole. "You're fucking gorgeous, all open and ready for me."

Pax pushed his ass back. "Brad, please."

Brad gave his ass a light slap. "Patience."

"How the fuck can you wait so long?"

"I know it will be worth it." And he did. The way Pax reacted to him was incredible, just like he'd imagined. His dick had been begging him to push into Pax's tight ass so he could feel it close around him ever since he'd gotten him on the bed, but he wanted Pax ready so he didn't have to hold back once he was buried inside him.

He rolled on a condom, slicked himself up, and then leaned over Pax's back. "I'm going to fuck you now, and you're not going to move until I tell you to."

"Shit" was Pax's ragged reply.

"You can make all the noise you want, though."

"Um, okay."

Brad ran his tongue along the outer edge of Pax's ear, making him shiver.

Then he rose up on his knees and gripped Pax's ass cheeks, pulling them apart. "This ass is mine."

"Yes." Pax's whispered agreement made his dick twitch.

He took hold of Pax's hips and pushed in just the tip of his cock.

Pax whimpered. "Need more."

"I'll give you more when I'm good and ready."

"Brad!"

"Don't move."

Pax was shaking with tension, but Brad only gave him a little more and then waited for his ass to adjust. Sweat dripped from Brad's face as he fought the urge to drive in.

"More," Pax begged.

But when he pushed past the tight ring of muscle, Pax tensed up. "You okay?"

"Just…need…a second."

"Easy. Take your time." Brad reached around and stroked Pax's cock while he waited.

"I want you."

"I know."

Brad waited until Pax was thrusting into his hand; then he gave him more and more, still moving slowly, but he didn't stop until he was all the way in.

"Yes! God, yes!" Pax said as Brad bottomed out.

"You love how I fill you up, don't you?"

"Yes, now move."

"Not yet."

Pax was practically vibrating. He turned

around to look at Brad. "Can't stay still. Dammit, Brad."

Brad grinned. "Fine. Move with me, then." He pulled out and drove in much harder than before.

"Yes!" Pax pushed back, trying to take even more.

Brad gave into the need to keep moving, increasing the power of his thrusts as Pax shoved back, obviously not wanting gentle anymore.

"So good. Brad, it's so good."

"Yeah, I know, baby."

Pax reached under himself to stroke his cock, but Brad pushed his hand away. "Let me."

He worked Pax's shaft in time to his strokes. Soon Pax tensed again, but this time Brad knew it was from pleasure not pain. "Come for me."

"Brad! Oh, God, Brad!" Pax shot his load then, coating Brad's hand with sticky fluid. Brad kept working him until he was done.

"Turn over," he ordered as he pulled out of Pax's ass.

Pax did, and their gazes met. Pax's expression was unguarded, open and soft, his face, neck, and chest flushed. He looked younger and so damn satisfied.

"Pax, I—" He stopped himself before he said too much.

Pax grinned drunkenly. "Yeah."

Brad laughed at how obvious it was that he was still floating from his climax. Then he stripped off the condom and took his cock in his hand.

Pax watched, his lower lip between his teeth as Brad worked himself faster and faster. "I want to cover you in my spunk."

"Yeah." Pax's mouth hung open. He was breathing almost as hard as Brad.

Brad was so close. Right there.

"Do it, Brad. I want it all over me."

"Fuck!" The first pulse of orgasm was so good it hurt. The pleasure went on and on until he wasn't sure it was ever going to stop. When it finally did, he sagged over Pax. He had to catch his breath before finally managing to flop down on his side.

"That was…"

"Amazing," Pax finished.

Neither of them said anything else for several seconds; then Brad propped himself on his elbow. "You were worth the wait."

Pax smiled. "You were too, but given the choice, I would gladly have been doing this years ago."

"Me too." What about years from now? Would Pax give him a chance to make this long term? "And I'm hoping this won't be the only time."

Pax's gaze skittered away. "We'll have prom night at least."

"And tomorrow."

"Right. Tomorrow too. And then you'll go back?"

"Not that quickly. I could stay for a bit. Work from here."

"Brad—"

Brad laid a finger on his lips. "Let's not try to figure that out now. Let's just enjoy this."

Pax nodded. "Okay."

"Shower?"

Pax glanced down at his come-covered abdomen. "Yeah, I need one."

"You do, and once we're in the shower I can get you messy and then clean you right up."

"Confident in your stamina, are you?"

"Are you saying you don't think I can make you come a third time?"

Pax shook his head. "I don't think that's possible."

"Why don't we find out?"

Pax smiled. "I'm good with that." Apparently his troubling thoughts were gone or at least pushed away for now. Sooner or later they'd have to confront their future, but Brad didn't see any problem with making Pax realize just how much fun they could have together first.

Chapter Fourteen

Pax scanned the day's schedule for the pottery store. What had he been thinking when Brad asked him to take the day off—that Brad's dick felt so damn good, he'd agree to anything to get more?

Cindy and Jada could handle it. He'd taken days off before. Once. Maybe twice. Only when he was extremely sick. But he was sure things would be fine as long as he went over everything with them.

The door jingled as Cindy walked in. Jada followed close behind her.

"Good morning!" he called. "I just have a few things to go over."

Cindy snatched the list from his hand. "No need. We'll be fine."

He reached for the piece of paper, but she stepped back.

"We need to go through the schedule."

"I looked over our calendar before I left the house."

Pax glared at her. "There are things I need to explain."

"I know you worry about this place."

"Too much," Jada added.

"But I want you to go have fun with your man and let us handle it."

"He's not—"

Both of them rolled their eyes as if they'd

rehearsed it.

"That man is yours if you want him to be," Jada said.

"How could you possibly know that?" Jada had only seen them together once, and she didn't know Brad at all.

"The way he looks at you." Once again they responded simultaneously.

Pax blew out a long breath. "If it's so obvious, how come no one else in town knows he's gay?"

Cindy snorted.

"What does that mean?" he asked.

"A lot of people suspect; they just aren't saying anything."

"Troy Anderson would've said something if he had any idea."

Jada wrinkled her nose. "Troy is an idiot. He couldn't understand a subtle clue if his life depended on it."

"Well, what about Trish? She didn't say anything."

Cindy laughed. "Of course Trish knows. She knows everything, including how wrong it would be for her to out him."

"How can you be sure?"

Cindy raised her brows and gave him a pointed look.

"Okay, fine. But that's Trish."

"I'm not saying everybody knows. Just people who are observant and wouldn't rule it out."

"Fine. Can we please go over the schedule now?"

Cindy looked down the list she'd taken from

him. "School group. Open the gallery. Deal with customers. Set up for the group tonight. We've got this."

Pax started to protest, but Cindy held up a hand. "Really. Just trust us."

"All right."

The door dinged again, and Brad stepped into the gallery. He was wearing shorts and a T-shirt that made his eyes look greener than usual. The outfit wasn't anything special, but somehow he looked amazing in it.

"See?" Jada said, nodding toward Brad.

"See what?" Brad asked.

Pax glowered at her. "Nothing. Let's get going."

"Are you brave enough to try Trish's again? I could really go for some biscuits and gravy."

"No good biscuits in Chicago?"

Brad laughed. "There are some places that try, but none of them compare to Trish's."

***

When they entered the diner, a table of women from Brad's high-school class beckoned him over. They'd been the "popular" girls, and they hadn't changed at all. Pax had no desire to get in on the conversation, so he found a booth and settled in.

A few moments later, Trish came over and set down two menus. "Coffee?"

"Yes, please."

She flipped over the cups on the table and filled them. "You seem a bit...rattled."

"It's been quite a week."

"A good one, though, right? Seeing Brad

again?"

Pax just nodded. This wasn't the time to go into the wide range of emotions seeing Brad had stirred up.

She glanced at Brad and then back to Pax. "I've got a feeling about this."

Uh-oh. Not one of Trish's feelings. "About what?"

"You and Brad."

"We're friends." Pax knew how lame that sounded as soon as the words left his mouth.

"Did I say differently?"

"Um…"

Trish winked. "Give him a chance. We'd all like to see you happy."

Pax snorted. "Plenty of people would like to see me gone."

"The ones who count want you to find someone."

"But Brad lives in Chicago."

Trish shrugged. But rather than dismissal or uncertainty, the gesture seemed to convey the sentiment "hush up, you know I'm right." How the hell did she do that? "It's just a feeling."

But those things never were with Trish. She had an uncanny ability to read people. Hell, some people were sure she had second sight.

Pax had wanted Brad for so long. So why was he terrified that people were pushing them together?

Because he was going to get his heart broken. Because he'd have to focus on something other than the gallery, and he'd have to— What? Actually live a life? Actually be Pax, not Paxton Marshall, artist and entrepreneur?

Yeah, that.

Brad extracted himself from the smiling group of women—good Lord, they were fawning over him as much as they had in high school, not that Pax blamed them. If they only knew what Brad could do in bed, they'd really go crazy. Pax couldn't help but feel a bit smug that he was all too aware of Brad's prowess.

Petty enough?

Why yes.

Brad slid into the booth across from him.

He looked worshipfully at his cup of coffee before taking a few long swallows. "I really needed this. I can't drink the sludge at the motel."

Pax wrinkled his nose. "I don't blame you."

Brad smiled. "It seems we have coffee snobbery in common."

"I don't think you can call that motel shit 'coffee.'"

Brad laughed. "What are you ordering?"

"I want French toast and bacon, but I should get a vegetarian egg-white omelet."

Brad narrowed his eyes. "Don't even think of getting something healthy."

His demanding tone reminded Pax of the night before. Damn, it had been hot having Brad tell him what to do. And now he was sitting in Trish's with a semi. *Great.*

Brad flipped through his menu. "When did Trish start serving healthy stuff?"

"Oh, she doesn't. But I don't always order off the menu."

"Good, I was getting nervous. I don't need Ames Bridge going all healthy hipster breakfast on me."

Pax laughed. "I can only imagine the look you'd get if you ordered avocado toast."

When Trish came back to take their orders, she didn't say anything about her "feeling" to Brad. Thank God.

Pax ordered the French toast, and Brad got biscuits and gravy with two eggs over easy.

"You boys need anything else?"

"No, ma'am," Brad said.

Trish was less that fifteen years older than Brad, and her brother Roscoe had graduated a year behind him, but that never stopped her from referring to men in their midthirties as boys. Pax would have found it annoying from anyone else, but Trish was just Trish and he loved her.

"Well, I hope we'll get more of a chance to talk while you're here," Trish said to Brad.

"Me too. I'm not sure how long I'll be in town."

"But you'll be back soon, right? At least that's what I heard."

Where did she hear that?

"I certainly don't intend to stay away long." He looked right at Pax as if making it clear that Pax was the reason he was there.

Trish gave Pax a knowing smirk. "I didn't think so."

"Tell me more about your art," Brad said after she walked away. "How do you find time for painting and glass-blowing when you're running the shop and the gallery?"

Pax sighed. "It's not easy."

"You're not skimping on your work, though, that's obvious. I looked at your website again, and you just keep improving."

Heat rushed to Pax's face. "Thank you. Having Cindy and Jada working for me helps a lot. I'll go paint in the studio while they run things. I'm there if there's an emergency, but at least I don't have to do all my art in the evenings."

"How do you pick the colors? Your paintings are… I don't know how to describe it, but they feel active, fluid, like the colors are actually swirling or pulsing."

His compliments were doing things to Pax that were soon going to render him unfit to be in public. Was it weird that he was getting hard from being told he was a good artist? "I love choosing colors. Cindy is good at that too. That's partly why I hired her. She took the first painting class I offered, and I saw right away how talented she was. She's great at helping the people who come in to paint pottery choose a color palette, and she can now teach basic painting to adults without my help. If I'm questioning my choices, I'll call her to see what she thinks."

Brad sighed. "As much as I'm loving working for myself, sometimes I really miss having someone to bounce ideas off of. I do call some of my old colleagues for consultations occasionally, but it's not the same."

"You're such an extrovert. It must get lonely."

"That's why I spend a lot of time at coffee

shops. I like having people around me."

Trish arrived with their food then. Pax hadn't realized how hungry he was until he took the first bite of French toast.

"Mmm. I always forget how good this is."

Brad just nodded. He seemed to be having a spiritual experience with his biscuits and gravy.

As they ate, Pax explained some painting techniques. Brad seemed far more fascinated that he would've expected.

Trish stopped by, refilled their coffee, and asked if they were ready for the check. As she walked away, Pax saw Cal headed their way.

"Mornin'," he said as he reached their booth.

Brad saluted him with his cup of coffee. "How are you?"

"Tired," Cal said. "How about you?"

"Fine now that I've got some caffeine."

Cal nodded. "I've polished off a pot at home, and I'm getting more here." Then he turned to Pax. "I've got a delivery out in the truck that I was gonna bring by your mama's house. Are you going by there today?"

"I can do that if you need me to take it to her."

"Yeah, that would be a big help. I'm running way behind on deliveries."

"Is everything okay?"

"Yeah," Cal said. "We had a mare give birth last night. She and the foal are doing fine, but I didn't get much sleep and my schedule is way off."

"You want me to grab the box now? We're about to head out anyway."

"That'd be great. I'm picking up a takeout

order, and then you can walk out with me."

When Cal headed to the counter, Pax glanced nervously at Brad. "I can just drop it off real quick. You don't have to visit my parents." Pax didn't need his mother trying to push them together. Although, surely his mom didn't suspect…

"I used to spend half my weekends at your house. It's not like I mind."

Oh, shit. "All right."

They got the box of produce and a bouquet of flowers from Cal and headed to Pax's parents' house. As Pax stepped through the side door into the kitchen, he called out, "Mom! Dad! I've got your delivery from McMurtry's, and Brad's with me."

"Brad Watson?" his mother asked.

"Yes, he's in town for the reunion."

"I remember. Come on through to the porch. I'm shucking corn."

Pax set the produce on the counter, and he and Brad walked through to the back porch.

"Wow, that's a lot of corn," Brad said. The basket in front of Pax's mother was huge.

"Elsie brought it over. It's from her neighbor's backyard, you know, the Marsdons."

Pax swallowed hard. He didn't want to think about that particular house. He still wasn't at all sure how he felt about Brad buying it. "But they moved."

"They did, but several of the neighbors are working together to keep up the garden until someone buys the place. There's so much corn, they can't eat it all."

"Well, don't tire yourself out," Pax said.

"Paxton, I've told you I am fine. I am fully

recovered."

She turned to Brad. "It's good to see you again. You hardly look any older than when you were in high school."

"You did see him at the funeral, Mom."

She glared at Pax. "I know that. You think I forget everything, but I don't. I'm really doing well."

His mom was right, but he worried anyway. If she pushed herself too hard, if she had another stroke, if he lost her too, he didn't know what he would do.

"You're looking very healthy, Miss Anne."

"Thank you. You always were a polite young man."

Pax fought the urge to roll his eyes.

"Paxton, are *you* okay? You look pale," his mother said.

He nodded, but Brad took his arm and guided him to a chair.

"Why don't you sit down? Is the heat getting you?"

"Oh Lord, it's been just awful this week," his mother said.

Brad smiled. "Yes, ma'am, it has."

"Dog days for sure. So tell me how you're doing, Brad."

As Pax tried to pull himself together, Brad talked about work and his shift to consulting.

"So you could live anywhere now, couldn't you?" Pax's mom said.

"I could." Brad gave Pax a meaningful look.

"Well, that's great," his mom said. "I'm so glad you're spending time with Pax while you're here. I know you were Rob's friend really, but you and Pax seemed rather close too."

Pax sputtered and tried to turn it into a cough. *Please don't let Mom be one of the ones who "knows" about me and Brad.*

Brad raised his brow at Pax's little coughing fit. "We were. I like to think we still are."

Pax's mother looked at him expectantly.

"Um… Yes. Yes, we are."

"Good," she said. "Did Cal send some flowers?"

Pax nodded. "Yes, ma'am. There's a lovely bouquet in the box. Do you want me to put it in a vase?"

"Yes, but in the plastic one we use for the cemetery. The flowers are for Rob's grave." She turned to Brad. "It will have been two years on Sunday."

"I'm so sorry, Miss Anne."

"We all are." She was silent for a few moments, but eventually she smiled again. "Would you boys mind taking those over for me?"

"I could do it later, Mom."

"Of course we will."

Their words ran over each other, and Pax bit back a groan. He did not want to go to the cemetery with Brad. Standing by Rob's grave together would be strange, creepy, awkward. But even worse, a lot of the older women in town—friends of his and Brad's parents—used the paths through the cemetery as a walking trail. No telling how many of them he and Brad would have to fend off. And for all he knew, they'd have a sixth sense like Cindy, Irene, and Trish. If he were lucky, the heat would deter most of them.

"See?" his mom said. "Brad doesn't mind."

Brad smiled. "That's right."

Bastard. "Mama—"

"I think it would be nice for you boys to go together." And she wasn't taking no for an answer.

"Yes, ma'am."

"And I hope y'all have some more plans before Brad leaves."

"We do," Brad said.

Pax tensed. Was he going to tell her about prom?

"Pax is going to one of the reunion activities with me."

That doesn't sound too bad.

"The prom?" his mother asked.

Pax wanted to sink through the floor. How did she even know about that?

"Um…yes, ma'am. That's right. I…um…"

She waved a hand. "Don't worry. I'm not shocked. I've learned you can't ever tell who's gay and who's not around here. Cal. You. Elsie's granddaughter Susan. And I don't know, but I think Ja—"

"Mama! Don't go spreading rumors. If you don't know—"

"Fine," she huffed. "But I'm only talking to you and Brad. It's not like I'm telling the whole town or anything."

Pax sighed. "I know, but—"

"Well, anyway, I'm thrilled for you two."

"Mom, we're just going out one evening. It's not—"

"Thank you," Brad said. "I'm honored to take

out your son."

Jesus, does he actually think we're back in high school?

"Paxton, why can't you have good manners like Brad?"

That's it. He had to get out of there. "We should go ahead and take the flowers. Where's Dad?"

"He took his truck over to Roscoe's. He said something was making a clanging sound. He ought to be back soon."

"All right. Call me if you need anything."

"I will. And I expect pictures from tomorrow night."

"Of course," Brad said.

Pax was going to kill him.

When they were settled in Brad's car with Pax holding the vase on his lap, Pax opened his mouth to tell Brad just what he thought of his attitude with Pax's mom, but Brad spoke before he could.

"Is it really so bad for your mom to know? She'd hear after tomorrow night anyway."

Brad was right, and Pax was probably being irrational. Still. "I was going to tell her before then, just not with you there."

"But Pax…"

His tone sounded ominous. "What?"

"Nothing."

Oh, shit. Was Brad hurt that Pax hadn't wanted him there? "It's not because—"

"It's fine."

"My mom is just… She's always on me to go out with someone. She worries because I don't date, and I don't want her putting pressure on you. On us."

"I don't feel any pressure, and I don't want this weekend to be the last time we spend together for another two or who knows how many years. I hope you feel the same way."

"I do." *And it scares the shit out of me.*

"Then what's—"

"Can we just deal with one difficult thing at a time?"

Brad's expression softened, and he reached over and laid a hand on top of Pax's. "Sure. I hadn't realized Sunday was the anniversary of Rob's passing. I knew it was around this time of year, but I hadn't thought about the dates."

"It's okay. You aren't expected to."

"I know this is a hard time for you and your parents. If there's anything I can do to make things easier…"

Pax shook his head. "Mom and Dad are doing a lot better. They don't talk about Rob as much, which—this may sound awful—is really good."

"That doesn't sound awful at all. Do you take flowers to his grave often?"

"No, my mom and dad usually go together. I… I don't like to. It's easier for me to remember him like he was when I'm not in front of a gravestone. I know a lot of people feel close to family or friends who've passed when they're at the cemetery, but I just feel sad."

"I can take them if you don't—"

"No, I think that this week especially, with you here, maybe I need to go. That probably sounds weird. But sometimes I'm not sure I've faced the reality of his being gone for good, even after all this time. It's more real when I'm there, which is probably why I don't like it."

"Well, just tell me if you need to go." Brad squeezed his hand. "I'm here for you."

"Thanks." Pax knew he meant that sincerely. Despite his own grief, Brad's main concern was for Pax. Why was he even questioning what he felt for this man?

***

Pax directed Brad to the right section of the graveyard. They parked at the curb, got out, and walked uphill to Rob's grave. There were already some flowers there, including a big wreath from the First Methodist Church, which his parents—and occasionally he—attended.

He set the vase down and squeezed his eyes shut. All the grief, all the things he would never get to do with Rob, all the things left unsaid, seemed to swirl around him. Tears stung his eyes. He really didn't want to cry there where anyone could see him.

Brad reached out and held his hand.

He started to pull away, but Brad held him firmly. "Let me do this."

His hand was warm, and Pax didn't really want to let go. Who cared if someone saw them? Even straight men touched when they were grieving.

"Thank you." The words were shaky.

"Pax, I miss him too."

Pax looked at him then, and Brad pulled him into a tight hug. Several long moments passed before they let go of each other.

"What would he say about us if he were here?" Brad asked.

"I don't know. I wish I did."

How could Pax go from grief to anger so fast? Now he wished Rob were there so he could tell him off for trying to cock-block him. But as he thought about it, he wondered… "Maybe that's what he wanted to tell me. He looked so upset, so sad. I thought it was because of the pain or that he knew he was dying, but what if he was sorry for what he said?"

Brad ran a hand over his hair and sighed. "I just have to believe he would've accepted us being together when he realized how much I care about you."

Pax nodded.

"Come on. Let's get out of here." They started down the hill, but someone called out.

"Brad Watson? Is that you? With Pax?"

It was Mrs. Jameson. Pax plastered a smile on his face and turned around. She'd been Brad and Rob's and then Pax's third-grade teacher. She was also a member of a deeply conservative church. If she'd seen them holding hands…

"It is me." Brad hugged her when she reached them.

"It's been too long since I've seen you."

"It has," Brad agreed.

"I guess you've come to pray for Rob. It must be hard on you being here."

She barely acknowledged Pax or any grief he might be feeling. She'd never been directly rude to him, but he knew she was uncomfortable being around him.

"I hear you may be moving back here."

Pax nearly choked. Trish being mildly psychic was one thing, but the rest of the town?

Brad looked almost as startled. "Um…"

"I saw you looking at the Marsdon place. Janet told me she'd love to sell to you. I bet she'd give you a good deal."

Brad hesitated, and Pax tensed. He might not be psychic like apparently half the women in this town, but he knew something was about to happen that he wasn't going to like.

"Actually she is. I've already put in an offer."

Chapter Fifteen

"You what?" The words slipped out before Pax could stop them.

Brad turned to him. "I…"

"Oh!" Mrs. Jameson gasped. "You didn't know? Well, of course you know the house, the one next to Elsie Nance's place."

Pax nodded mechanically, managing to hold all his screaming inside.

"It will sure be nice to have such a good man back among us."

Oh, just wait until you hear.

"I know your parents were Methodists, but we'd love to have you at the Tabernacle."

"Um…I…"

Pax would've found Brad's stumbling attempt to tell her no way in hell would he set foot in that place funny if he hadn't been so angry, scared, and slightly dizzy from finding out that Brad had gone ahead with buying the house after promising they could talk more about it.

Mrs. Jameson glanced at her watch then. "Oooh, I've got to run. We teachers have a lunch meeting today so we can talk about the new year. I can't believe how soon school will be starting."

"It was nice to see you," Brad said.

"You too. I can't wait to tell everyone."

"Oh, actually, it's—"

But she'd already dashed off.

"I suppose that will be all over town in a few minutes. If it isn't already. Was I going to be the last to hear?"

"The agent said someone else was interested in the property. She thought they might put in an offer soon, and I didn't want to lose the chance. Nothing is settled yet."

"You know they'll accept. They wanted to sell to you."

"Yes, but I need to have it inspected, and buying it doesn't mean I'm going to live there. I told you I was already considering it before I saw you again."

Pax nodded. He had a hell of a lot more to say, but making a scene at the cemetery would only make things worse.

But Brad continued to push things. "And if I do want to own a place here, I might not find anything else."

"Right, because the Ames Bridge housing market is so hot."

Brad's eyes widened. Likely he was surprised by the amount of venom in Pax's words. Even Pax was a little shocked.

"I mean a place where I know the neighbors on both sides are supportive."

He did have a point. "You said we'd talk about it."

"And we can."

Pax lowered his voice to barely a whisper. "I may like to be told what to do in bed, but I don't like other people making decisions for me."

"That's not what this is!" Brad was getting angry, his jaw tight, his eyes dark like they were when he'd fucked Pax.

"Yes, it is. You said you wouldn't force this."

"I haven't forced anything!" Now Brad was shouting.

"People are staring."

"I don't give a fuck about them."

Pax blew out a long breath. "You obviously do since you still haven't told anyone here that you're gay."

Brad's mouth dropped open.

Shit, Pax had gone too far.

"You know what? You're right. I haven't. But would that've made a difference?"

"I don't know; maybe. I just think once you see what it's like to be out in this town, you'll change your mind. You're not used to being in a place where people who've known you your whole life critique everything you do."

Brad shook his head. "You're right. I don't have people watching me like that in Chicago. That's why I wanted to get away to a bigger place. I thought it would make me happy, but it didn't."

"Really?" Pax was having a hard time believing that.

"No, having one life there and a different life when I talked to my parents or other people who knew me before I moved... That sucked. Of course, I love certain aspects of living in a big city. I'm sure you enjoyed having more freedom in Savannah."

Pax nodded. "I did, but it was still Georgia."

"And there are plenty of homophobic assholes

everywhere. Don't think I haven't had to deal with that just because I got out of the South."

Pax was probably being far too dismissive of what Brad had faced. "I know. It's just different being in the place where you grew up. I don't want you making promises because…"

"Because why?"

The words rushed out before he could stop them. "Because I don't want to get hurt."

"So it's not worth taking a risk with me?"

"That's not…"

"I wish I could promise that neither of us will get hurt, but I can't, no one can, and I won't lie to you."

"Brad, I didn't mean it like that."

"But you did."

Shit. Pax couldn't keep arguing, because Brad was partly right.

Brad started walking toward the car. "Come on. I'll drive you back."

"I can walk from here."

Brad turned back to him. "Pax, you don't have to."

"I doubt it's even a mile, and it's not that hot yet. I'm perfectly capable of walking."

"But I… Fine."

Brad left him standing there. After a few seconds, Pax started walking in the other direction as fast as he could, as if maybe he could outrun the tears burning his eyes. He didn't bother looking around the cemetery; it was almost guaranteed someone had watched them argue. Now that would be all over town too. Perfect.

His walk took him by Central Bakery, one of his favorite places in town. The sweet smell of their icing—the best icing he'd ever had—wafted out to him. He needed one of his favorite cookies. The gingerbread ones covered in a thick layer of icing. They were exquisite, and he hadn't let himself indulge in one in weeks. If there was ever a day to stuff his face with sugar, this was it.

He was surprised to see Trish's niece Lucy behind the counter.

"Good morning," she called when he stepped into the blessed air-conditioning.

He forced himself to smile. He was going to have to act like everything was fine if he didn't want more questions and rumors.

Brad is buying a house. A house in Ames Bridge.

"I didn't realize you were working here." His voice sounded almost normal.

"I just started a few weeks ago. I signed up for some classes at the community college. I'm going to do the pastry arts certificate there."

"That's fantastic. I know you've been trying to decide what you wanted to do. Are you still working at the feed store too?"

"Nope. I might work a shift or two at the diner if Trish really needs me, but otherwise, it's this and school until I graduate. I told my parents I'd pay for school myself, but I'm not working there anymore. I need to branch out."

Pax nodded. "I think this is great, and I want to sample some of your baking."

"I made these today." She pointed to the

shortbread in the cookie case. "There's chocolate and the traditional ones."

"I'll take two of each and two of the iced flowers."

She grinned. "You got it."

As Lucy packed up the cookies, Pax looked around at the other items for sale. Then Paula, the owner, came out from the back with a three-tiered wedding cake.

"Wow. That's gorgeous," Pax said.

"It's for a couple over in Lexington. He used to live here, though. That's why they hired us. Benjamin Worth? Did you know him?"

"Of course. He was a year or two older than my brother."

"That's right," Paula said. "Well, he's finally marrying a girl he's known since they were babies. She lived next door to his grandparents, and she was his first crush. Can you imagine after all these years?"

He had to clear his throat before he could answer. "Um… Yeah. That's amazing."

She studied him for a moment. "Are you okay?"

He nodded, probably a bit more frantically than he should. "I've just had a crazy morning."

"Well, take care in this heat."

The weather. That was a nice, safe topic, unlikely to make him look like a maniac. "I hear it might cool off some this weekend."

"I hope so." Paula removed a shelf so she could place the cake in the massive fridge, and Lucy set his bag on the counter and rang him up.

Once he'd paid, he walked quickly toward the

gallery. He entered from the back door and went right up the steps to his apartment. He didn't even peek to see how things were going. Cindy and Jada were right; they could handle it. And right then, all he was capable of was dragging himself up the stairs and then stuffing cookies in his face.

He flopped down on the sofa in his tiny living room/kitchen. The space had seemed fine for him, plenty large enough until he started thinking about having Brad over. He'd never had a man stay there. What would it be like if Brad lived in the Marsdon house? They'd—he'd—have plenty of space then. The house was a huge Victorian farmhouse with an amazing front porch—where Miss Elsie could watch their every move. The thing he loved best about this apartment was that no one could spy on him, no one bothered him, no one visited. He was utterly alone.

That was a good thing, wasn't it? It used to be.

The Marsdon house was right in the middle of gossip central, on one of the town's main streets. How would that be better?

Why was he even thinking about living with Brad? He hadn't mentioned Pax moving in with him when he'd talked about buying the place.

Pax opened the bakery bag and breathed deeply. He'd associated the scent of Central Bakery with comfort for as long as he could remember. He lifted out one of the iced flowers and took a big bite. Fuck people who said you shouldn't self-medicate with food. It was a hell of a lot better than other things he could do.

By the time he'd finished the first cookie, he remembered he couldn't eat quite as much of that rich icing as he used to be able to. He'd save the other cookies for later. After setting the bag on the chest he used for a coffee table, he lay back on the couch. What the fuck was he going to do now?

He must have drifted off to sleep, because he awoke to the sound of his phone buzzing with a text from Brad.

I'm sorry. Can we talk?

Suddenly, he wanted Brad there more than anything. *Yes. Come to the gallery. Park in back. Text me and I'll let you in.*

Five minutes later Pax got another text. *I'm here.*

He took the steps two at a time. After practically running away from Brad, he was now running toward him as fast as he could. Was he fucked up or what?

When he reached the door, he yanked it open and pulled Brad inside. Brad enveloped him in a tight hug. Then Pax led the way to his apartment.

"You want to sit down?" Pax gestured toward the sofa. "I have cookies. I could make coffee or get you a water or…"

"You don't have to go to this stupid prom if you don't want to."

The anguish on Brad's face made nausea curl in Pax's stomach. "No! I want to."

"You'll end up in the middle of all the shit that'll come down on me."

"After all the times you stood up for me back when we were kids, you think I'm going to let you do this alone? You're crazy. No matter what happens afterward, whether you stay here or don't, whether we…whether there's anything more between us…"

"You really have to ask if there is?"

"Um… I…"

Brad blew out a long breath. "Pax."

"Still here."

"Do you really want me to leave after tomorrow night?"

Instead of rushing in with an answer, Pax gave himself a moment to think. Finally, he said, "No, but I'm scared for you to stay."

Brad took a step toward him.

"Kiss me," Pax begged.

Brad cupped his face in both hands. "Pax, I want you just as much now as I did in high school, as I did when I saw you two years ago, as I did last night. I care about you. A lot. And I don't want this to end after tomorrow."

"I don't either."

"Then can we… What are you willing to give?"

Everything. My soul. "Are you really moving here?"

Brad held his gaze. "That doesn't answer my question."

"I'm willing to…date you? Would that even be the right term? I could be your boyfriend, your partner, but how do we do that?"

"Just like everyone else."

"But we're not…"

"We're a couple just like a man and a woman or any two people who don't have a whole town in their business."

"But that's not what we are."

"Pax."

He sighed. "Okay, I'll try."

"You will? Truly?"

Pax nodded. "Yes, so can you kiss me now?"

Brad laughed and then did exactly that.

***

Brad had come to Pax's apartment thinking he might have to walk away without ever touching Pax again. Now that Pax was in his arms again, he was so consumed with need, he could hardly think.

"Want you," he whispered.

Pax pressed against him, and Brad gripped his ass, holding them together.

"Come on." He tugged Pax, and they stumbled, nearly falling over the coffee table in their attempt to reach the couch without letting go of each other.

"Bed. In there." Pax pointed toward the doorway that clearly led to his bedroom, but Brad ignored him.

"Can't move that far," he said as he fell backward onto the couch, pulling Pax down on top of him.

He bent one knee, setting his other foot on the floor, so Pax could settle between his legs. Pax sucked on his bottom lip as they ground against each other. The friction felt incredible.

"Feels so fucking good," Pax said, the words breathless.

"Damn right it does."

Brad wanted to strip him so he could fuck him again, but this was so good that he couldn't make himself stop.

Finally Pax pulled away and tried to shift back on his knees, nearly falling off the couch in the process.

Brad reached for him. "Come back."

Pax ignored him as he undid Brad's pants enough to free his cock. Then he leaned down and took it in his mouth. Brad lost the ability to speak. He wasn't sure he even remembered how to breathe, because Pax wasn't the least bit tentative. He swallowed Brad's length and sucked so hard, Brad thought he would pass out from the pleasure. He resisted holding Pax's head where he wanted him, but he bucked up, pushing himself even deeper. Pax didn't seem to mind. He moaned around Brad's shaft, taking everything Brad gave, sucking, licking, working him over until he was right at the edge.

"Pax, I... I'm going to..."

Pax looked up at Brad and smiled around his shaft. That was all it took to send Brad over. When he finished and sagged against the couch, Pax sat back and licked his lips.

"Damn, that was amazing."

Pax grinned. "Yeah, it was."

"Come here. It's your turn," Brad said, but Pax shook his head. Brad looked down and realized that at some point Pax had freed his own cock and his hand was now sticky with come.

"Let me clean you up, then," he said, taking hold of Pax's wrist.

Pax shifted so Brad could pull Pax's hand to his mouth. He ran his tongue over each finger and then swiped it over his palm.

"Fuck." The word whooshed out of Pax like

an exhalation.

Brad chuckled. "Too soon for that."

He pulled Pax down until his head was pillowed on Brad's chest. The couch wasn't really big enough for the two of them, but no way in hell was he moving anytime soon.

After a few moments of silence, he glanced around. "Why do I smell icing?"

"I got cookies." Pax pointed to a white paper bag that lay on the floor. Central Bakery was stamped on the side.

Brad vaguely remembered the bag being on the coffee table when he'd arrived. He reached out and snagged the edge so he could pull it toward them. When he looked inside, he frowned. "I think we kind of destroyed them."

"They'll still taste good."

Brad laughed. "That sounds like the voice of experience."

"Yeah, it is. The iced ones are my favorite, and Lucy—you remember Lucy Simpkins, Trish's niece, her older brother's kid?"

He frowned. "Maybe, but all those nieces and nephews were babies when I left for college."

"I guess that's right. She's only nineteen, so she wouldn't even have been born then. Anyway, she's going to culinary school, and she made the shortbread."

Brad pulled out a piece that looked like it must be chocolate and took a bite. "Mmm. That is good."

"I haven't tried it yet," Pax said.

Brad brought what was left of the cookie to

Pax's lips. Pax took it into his mouth and then licked the crumbs off Brad's fingers.

He smiled as he chewed. "Wow, that is good."

Next Brad fed him a piece of the iced cookie. Some icing stuck to his lips, and Brad proceeded to lick it off. When he finished, Pax took hold of his wrist and cleaned his fingers very thoroughly.

"Keep that up, and we're going to have round two sooner rather than later."

Pax grinned wickedly as he drew out a piece with especially thick icing. This time he deliberately rubbed it on his lips before eating it.

Brad growled and pulled Pax to him for a harsh but sweet-tasting kiss.

"Tease," he muttered.

"You love it."

Brad laughed. "I do. You want to see just how much?"

"Yes, but maybe on the bed this time."

Brad sat up fast, and Pax tumbled to the floor. They laughed so hard that it took them a while to make it to the bedroom, but once they got there, they didn't leave except to order pizza. They ate and talked until it was time for Brad to go to a reunion trivia night, the first of the official Welcome Back Class of 1997 events.

Chapter Sixteen

As Pax pulled up at the Boathouse, where they were having dinner before the prom, he couldn't decide if he was excited or scared to death. As good as everything had been between them the day before, they'd never talked more specifically about what their future would mean.

Was Brad seriously moving here? Would he keep an apartment in Chicago? Being able to afford such a thing baffled Pax, but Brad had said he could make it work. How often would he be here? What would he think after tonight, after everyone knew? And then the word would spread, and more people would know, and more shit would come down on him—on both of them—but Pax wasn't going to back down. He'd made a promise, and after he championed Cal and Beck's relationship, he'd be a hell of a hypocrite to beg Brad to keep their—whatever it was—secret.

It's a relationship.

It's two friends with good sexual chemistry, who don't really know each other as adults yet.

It's two men who love each other.

No. I can't be in love with him already.

Already? It's been twenty years.

During most of which I haven't seen him.

No one really changes that much after high school. That's why reunions are so shitty. It's all just like it was, every sickening bit of it.

And all those issues—Pax imagined Brad was thinking about at least some of them too—meant that their conversation over dinner was at best stilted and at worst really fucking awkward.

"Are you sure you want to go through with this?" Brad asked when the waiter took his credit card and headed off to process it.

Pax frowned. "Are you?"

"Yes."

"Then I'm with you. I told you that." He was, but the closer they got to the moment when they'd walk into Ames Bridge High, the more butterflies joined the dance in his stomach. There were so many now, he hadn't been able to eat more than a bite of the crème brûlée they were supposed to be splitting.

Brad sighed. "Then why do you seem so…"

"Scared?"

"Yeah."

"Because I am. Isn't that why you seem so walled off tonight?"

Brad gave him a sheepish look. "I'd hoped my nerves weren't that obvious. I'm just trying to prepare myself. When I was back in Chicago, everything seemed so clear. I'd come here, tell people I was gay. They could react however they wanted. I'd ignore their shit, see if I had a chance with you, and—"

Pax's eyes widened. "Wait. You planned that?"

"What?"

"To…pursue me."

Brad nodded. "I did make a lunch date with you weeks before I came."

"But I thought that was just you seeing an old friend."

He shrugged. "It might've been nothing more than that if you weren't interested, but…"

"I was. I am."

"Does it bother you that I planned it, like my buying a house?"

Pax shook his head as heat rose in his cheeks. "No, it's…actually kinda hot."

Brad laughed. "Good."

"Now you seem more like yourself."

"Overconfident?"

"Playful."

He laid his hand over Brad's, not giving a fuck who saw. "I know this is going to suck."

"Yeah, but it's the right thing to do."

Pax just hoped Brad hadn't underestimated how shitty people could be.

Maybe you're actually underestimating the support of others, just like Cal did.

He'd have to hold on to that thought.

***

Due to misplaced nostalgia or a lack of contributions to the reunion fund, the "prom" was being held in the high-school gym. A long line of cars snaked through the high-school parking lot as drivers let their passengers out, then searched for spots in the small lot closest to the south entrance. Pax desperately needed to use the restroom after consuming a gallon of iced tea at dinner. He'd decided that while alcohol might help him brush off the nasty comments they'd no doubt receive, getting drunk on such a big night would be a mistake.

Besides, Brad would need the comfort of alcohol more than he did. It was best if he stayed sober so he could drive them home.

"I should've gone to the bathroom before we left the restaurant," he said.

"Why don't we switch? You can go and then meet me by the doors."

Pax didn't want to face the crowd alone, but he was getting desperate, so he circled close to the entrance, stopped the car, and hopped out, leaving Brad to find a parking place. He managed to slip into the school without having to talk to anyone. Thankfully, the restrooms on the side of the gym close to the classrooms were open. As he'd guessed, there was no one by them. Most people would go to the ones closer to the main entrance.

When he came out of the restroom and stepped back outside, his luck changed. A large group of people congregated there just as they'd been in the mornings before school all those years ago.

"Hey, Pax, what are you doing here?"

Shit, it was Troy, the last person he wanted to see. Pax fought the urge to comment on how absurd Troy looked in a camo tux with a cowboy hat. Where did a person even rent such a monstrosity?

"I'm here with Brad," Pax said, looking toward the parking lot, hoping to see Brad headed his way.

A guy Pax remembered as being particularly obnoxious laughed. "What did you do? Take him for your team?"

Troy punched his friend in the arm. "Like that would happen."

"Actually—"

Pax was prevented from saying anything else by the arrival of two women, one of whom appeared to be married to the jerk whose name he'd forgotten. He hoped the other woman didn't have the misfortune of being Troy's date.

"We've been waiting in there for ages," what's-his-name's wife said.

The asshole snarled at her. "I needed a cigarette. Why did we even come to this dumb thing anyway?"

"Don't you want to see everyone?" she asked, looking at him like he was crazy.

"No. Anyone worth seeing I already see all the time anyway."

Finally, he'd said something Pax could agree with.

"Where's your jacket?" the woman demanded.

"I left it in the car."

"Then go get it."

Troy snickered. "I told you she'd notice."

The man's wife scowled. "This is a formal event; you have to wear the jacket."

"Real cowboys don't have to wear all this crap," Troy argued.

Real cowboys don't wear camo either. Pax fought to keep his face neutral as he winced inwardly.

The woman rolled her eyes. "Just go get it."

By the time they finished arguing, Brad was headed their way. Pax couldn't help but stare at him as he approached. He was fairly sure Troy or one of the others had said something to him, but he didn't hear it. Brad had actually rented a tux instead of wearing a suit like a lot of the men. The design was classic, all black except for the stark white shirt. He'd cowboyed it up by wearing a bolo and a black Stetson. His broad shoulders and thick thighs strained against the tuxedo's fabric. He was a walking wet dream. Pax was certain Brad would inspire a cowboy fetish in just about anybody, except maybe the assholes Pax was standing with. He finally tore his gaze from Brad and looked over at them. Both women were staring at Brad, their lips parted, their eyes bright. *Sorry, ladies, he's taken.*

What was with this smug, possessive streak?

"Brad!" The asshole yelled when Brad was still too far away for civil conversation.

"Hi, Luther." Brad gave a half-hearted wave.

Luther. That was his name. Pax remembered him now. His brother Mark had been in Pax's class. Mark had been fond of calling Pax a fag long before Pax had even known he liked guys.

"Pax says he's with you. What's that about?" Luther asked.

Brad walked right up to Pax and put his arm around him. "I asked him to come with me."

"Because you missed Rob or what?" Troy asked.

"No, because I missed Pax and I wanted him to be my date."

Troy's mouth fell open, and Luther took a step back.

"You're a fucking queer?" Troy asked.

"No way," Luther said, their words running together.

Brad took Pax's arm, and without saying

another word, they walked past the gaping idiots and into the school. Pax practically had to run to keep pace with Brad. He had wondered earlier if Brad would come right out and say he was gay at the start of the evening or if they'd slowly let people get the idea. Now he had his answer.

"You realize the whole class will know about you within two minutes," he whispered.

"Yeah, in a way it was easier to tell those losers first. They'll spread the story fast, and then less people will ask us stupid questions."

Pax squeezed his arm. "Are you okay with all this?"

"It's too late to take it back now." He laid his hand over Pax's.

"We don't have to stay long."

Brad turned to him and lifted his brows. "No way in hell am I going to miss out on a chance to dance with my man when he's wearing his cowboy getup."

Pax grinned. *His man.* He liked that more than he should.

He squeezed Brad's hand as they walked through the fake saloon doors into the gym. They both stopped to look around. As far as Pax could tell, it was 1989 all over again, just with a little less big hair and a lot more alcohol out in the open.

Numerous cardboard cactuses were placed strategically around the room, and there was a photo booth where attendees could stand behind a cutout of some Old West gunslingers. A man and a woman waved at him and Brad. It took Pax a few moments to recognize them. They'd been friends of Rob's from the drama club, ones Pax knew vaguely but never hung out with. They motioned him over.

"Remind me of their names," Brad whispered.

"Mandy and Krishna. They'll be part of the supportive crowd."

He studied them as they approached. Mandy was wearing a scandalously short—for Ames Bridge, anyway—cowgirl dress, with what must have been pounds of rhinestones, and a glittering red cowgirl hat. He admired her daring. Krishna must have borrowed his clothes; his suit hung loosely, but from the way he was shifting from one foot to the other, Pax was sure his cowboy boots must be at least a size too small.

He and Brad passed the bar on their way across the gym. "Do you mind if I get a drink and then join you?" Brad asked.

"Go ahead. I bet the drink tickets are the only thing luring most of these people here."

"I'm sure you're right. Back in high school, all we had was lime-sherbet punch, not that plenty of us didn't doctor it. Those deep jacket pockets were perfect for hiding a flask."

Pax laughed. "I bet."

Krishna looked quizzically toward Brad's retreating form as Pax walked over to him. "Was that Brad Watson?"

"Yeah."

Mandy grinned. "That's sweet. He always thought the world of you."

Pax looked at her, uncertain. "Really?"

"Sure. He had a terrible crush on you, but I doubt anyone else picked up on it."

Krishna looked stunned. "What?"

His words collided with Pax's. "You knew?"

"After I realized I liked girls, I was more likely to notice when someone else was different."

Pax had forgotten that he'd seen a newspaper picture of Mandy with her partner at a Winston-Salem pride event.

"Wait a minute," Krishna said. "You're telling me Brad is gay?"

"Yes," Mandy answered.

Krishna looked at Pax as if he needed confirmation.

"He is," Pax confirmed.

"So you're here as his date, not just his friend?"

Pax nodded.

Mandy squeezed his arm. "That is so sweet. I'm so glad you two finally got together."

"We're not really together." Pax immediately felt like he'd said the wrong thing. He didn't want people assuming anything, but he'd told Brad he'd give their relationship a try. "He's got to go back to Chicago."

Brad came up behind him then. "Eventually," he said.

"What?" Mandy asked.

"I eventually have to go back to Chicago; not right away."

So he had heard what Pax had said. Damn, he'd have to apologize later.

Mandy held out her hand to Brad. "Do you remember me? I'm Mandy Thompson."

"Of course I do," Brad said as they shook.

"My partner, Rose, is over there." Mandy pointed at a woman with long red hair, who was dancing like no one was watching.

Brad's eyes widened for a moment, and then he smiled. "I'm glad she could be here with you."

Pax watched her dance for a moment. "Wow, she's vivacious."

Mandy lifted her brows suggestively. "She sure is."

"Whoa!" Krishna held up his hands. "TMI."

Mandy slapped his arm. "You hush."

Brad laughed, that deep, rich, swoon-worthy sound Pax loved so much. Pax smiled up at him, not caring if Mandy and Krishna saw how much Pax wanted him.

Brad set his drink on a nearby table. "Let's dance."

"See you later," Pax called over his shoulder as he followed Brad to the dance floor. Plenty of heads turned as they walked by, and there were lots of whispered conversations once they'd passed. Some of them carried ugly insults, others titillation. But once he and Brad started dancing, Pax forgot about everything but watching Brad move. He had more grace than a man his size should.

Pax lost himself in the nostalgic music for a while. They were too close to the speakers for conversation, but Brad held up a finger, asking him to wait. He disappeared into the crowd and returned a few minutes later. Pax raised his brows in question, but Brad just grinned.

"Open Your Heart" started to play a few seconds later, and Pax stared at Brad in disbelief.

Brad shrugged and leaned down so he could whisper-shout in Pax's ear. "I remember how much you liked this one."

Pax laughed. "I made Rob so sick of it, he threatened to smash my CD player."

Brad moved closer as the song played. By the end he was rubbing up on Pax, and people were openly staring. Mandy caught Pax's eye and winked. Then she grabbed her partner by the hips and ground against her. Several other couples were being just as intimate, but since they were het, no one looked askance at them. Pax made a mental note to contact Mandy soon. He assumed she still lived in Winston, and that was close enough for them to get to know each other better.

By the time the song ended, he and Brad were both dripping with sweat. The air-conditioning in the gym had always been shit, and tonight was no exception.

***

Brad fanned himself. "Whew! It's hot. You ready for a break?"

Pax nodded. They walked off the dance floor and peeled out of their jackets as many of the men had already done. He took Pax's and laid it and his own over the back of a chair.

"I need some water. You want another drink?" Pax asked.

Before Brad could answer, someone came up behind them. "What the fuck is this?"

Great. It was Troy.

"It's exactly what you think it is." Brad's tone was more belligerent than was probably wise.

Troy turned to Pax and narrowed his eyes. "How the fuck did you do it?"

"Do what?" Pax asked.

Brad fought the urge to step in front of Pax. He didn't need a protector, though Brad sure as hell was willing to be one.

Troy snorted. "Turn Brad gay."

"Brad's sexuality isn't something I or anyone else has the power to change."

Troy wrinkled his nose and looked back at Brad. "No way in hell were you gay when we were in high school."

Troy was talking so damn loud that a crowd had gathered around them. Most of them were nodding like they agreed with Troy, but he did see Mandy, Rose, and Krishna standing off to the side. "I was every bit as gay then as I am now."

"But we went out together," Troy said.

Brad raised his brows.

"With girls!" Troy's voice went up on the last words. "Double dates."

Brad bit back a laugh, but Pax looked uneasy. More people were circling around them. He noticed Scott and Jack standing together. Scott looked almost as disbelieving as Troy. Jack's expression was too bland not to be masking something. Was it support or anger?

"All the girls were hot for you," Marcie added. She was one of the former cheerleaders who'd talked to him in Trish's the day before.

He doubted this was the time to explain that what women felt for him had nothing to do with whether he wanted them or not.

"If you were a fucking queer, what were you doing taking all the girls from us?" Luther yelled.

Right, because it was all about Luther and others like him.

Luther took a step forward. He'd clearly had a lot to drink. For the first time Brad worried things would turn violent. He needed to diffuse this fast.

"I didn't tell anyone in high school because I expected most people would react like you are now, or worse. But I'm saying it now. I'm gay, and I'm dating Pax." He looked back and forth from Troy to Luther. "Let's all get back to dancing."

"I don't want to dance with faggots," Luther said.

His wife linked her arm with his and tugged. "Quit being an ass. They aren't dancing anyway."

"How many more of you are here?" Luther yelled, looking toward Mandy and Rose.

No way in hell was Brad letting him drag them into this. He'd let Luther's and Troy's crap slide in high school. He was done with that now. "Back off."

Luther snarled. "Come to think of it, you always did stand up for fucking homos like Pax back in high school. I thought you were just soft, but now I know what you were up to."

"That's enough." His wife pulled on his arm again.

He yanked himself loose, but thank God, he didn't come at Brad.

"I'm leaving," he announced loudly. "I didn't want to come to this fucking thing anyway, and now that it's all about rainbows and butt fuckers, I'm out of here."

"Good riddance," Pax whispered.

Brad watched Luther stomp off, then turned to Pax. "I thought I was going to have to lay him out for a minute there."

Pax nodded. "Me too."

Someone dropped a hand on Brad's shoulder. He turned, ready to defend himself, but it was Jack.

He held out his hand for Brad to shake. "I want you to know that not everyone feels like that."

"Thanks," Brad accepted the handshake.

"That goes for me too," Scott said.

That one surprised him a lot more, but Jack laughed. "Your mama'd rip you to pieces if she caught you acting like those idiots."

"She would," Scott agreed.

Jack nodded. "That's because she raised you right. 'Don't be an asshole' is her number-one rule."

"She didn't phrase it quite like that when we were kids, but that's exactly what she meant."

"Only because if she had, you'd have called her on it and said if she could talk like that, you could too," Jack added.

"And then I'd have gotten my ass beat and been sent to my room for a year."

They all laughed, except for Pax. He stood to the side, stiffly, observing them.

"Seriously, though, I don't know about all this"—Scott gestured between Brad and Pax—"but you were a good friend, and I'm not going to say anything against you now."

Brad nodded. "Thank you."

Scott looked at Pax then. "Or you. Mama

adores you, and you've done a lot for Ames Bridge, for tourism and the arts and stuff."

"Thank you." Pax smiled, but it didn't reach his eyes. Brad could feel waves of tension coming off him.

"I'm going to get a drink." Jack waved toward the bar. "Anyone need anything?"

Pax and Brad shook their heads, even though Pax had just mentioned needing water.

"I'll go with you," Scott said.

The rest of the onlookers had dispersed by the time Jack and Scott walked off, so Brad turned to Pax. "You still want some water?"

"Yeah, but I need to go to the bathroom too. I… I'll be back."

He dashed away before Brad could say anything else. Even though he'd participated in the conversation with Scott and Jack, Brad had felt him withdrawing, building back barriers he'd let down on the dance floor. Brad wanted to go back to grinding and forget about stupid assholes like Luther and Troy.

But a few moments later, Brad saw his favorite high-school teacher, Mrs. Sheffield, across the room. She'd taught him algebra and trigonometry and given him the confidence he needed to go into computer engineering. He pulled out his phone and texted Pax.

I'm going to walk around. Text me if you can't find me.

"How are you, Mrs. Sheffield?" he asked when he reached the group of teachers she stood with.

She turned, but rather than the smile he was expecting, she pursed her lips. "Brad."

That was all she said, but the word conveyed disgust and disappointment.

"Um…" Brad had been going to thank her for being an inspiration to him, but now…

"I'm sorry. I've got to go." She turned and walked away without another word to him.

He stared after her for a few seconds. When he turned back to the group she'd been with, several of the women looked incredibly uncomfortable, but one, Mrs. Spindale, an English teacher he'd despised, addressed him. "She doesn't believe in all this homosexual stuff. It was a terrible shock to hear you'd been seduced by that Paxton Marshall. She prays for him every night; I'm sure she'll pray for you too."

"Right." As if that made it okay. He was going to get prayers, so he shouldn't mind being insulted? Was that it?

His stomach churned as he walked away. He needed a drink, badly. But he wasn't certain it would stay down. So instead he stepped outside, hoping a breath of fresh air might return some of his equilibrium.

Unfortunately, fresh air was in short supply. There were far more people in the courtyard than he'd expected, and most of them were smoking. He wandered, trying to find a place where the air wasn't heavy with cigarette smoke.

Finally, he found an unoccupied spot along the breezeway that connected the older part of the school to the new building that housed the gym. After a few moments of looking up at the stars and taking slow, deep breaths, a conversation happening back in the courtyard drew his attention.

"Can you believe it?" a woman asked.

"No, I'm horrified," a man responded. "I used to shower with him."

"Gross!" she said, and Brad could hear the shudder in her voice. "He was probably looking at your dick the whole time."

"I know. And I heard he's moving back here."

There was no doubt they were talking about him.

"Like we need more of that in this town."

So much for clean air. Apparently these two thought he dirtied it just by existing.

He moved to where he could see the couple. The man, Wilson, had played baseball with Brad, and his companion, Laura, had happily let him borrow her notes when he'd had to leave chemistry early for games. He'd never been close to Wilson, but from what he remembered, the guy had been known as the king of beer pong and had attempted to set a record for pissing off the most women with his assumption that they all wanted to sleep with him. How had he become such a righteous prig?

There were many things he wanted to say to them, like reminding Wilson of his high school "glory" days, but he just walked away because if he opened his mouth, he wasn't sure he could keep his voice steady. The last thing he wanted was for them to know how much they'd affected him.

How had he thought it wouldn't hurt to have people he knew turn against him? He'd honestly thought he could dismiss it as long as he had Pax by his side. Now he knew Pax had been right. It was painful as hell.

Where *was* Pax? He'd had plenty of time to go to the bathroom and get a bottle of water by now.

He pulled out his phone. No message. Maybe Pax had given up on him too.

He considered calling someone to pick him up since they'd taken Pax's car—Cal? Irene? Pax's mother? That would be interesting, but it also wouldn't be right. He wasn't going to run out on Pax. He stepped back inside and started looking for him in the crowd.

Silvia Violet

Chapter Seventeen

When Pax walked away from Brad, he headed straight for the bathroom he'd used when they first arrived. Once again, it was blessedly empty. He leaned against the counter and took a deep breath. He was physically worn out from dancing, which reminded him he still hadn't managed to start a regular workout routine. But the ache in his legs was nothing compared to the emotional exhaustion.

The look on Brad's face when Luther said that about dancing with fags...

It had broken Pax's heart. Brad looked so stunned, so crushed. He'd covered it quickly with anger, but Pax had seen the startled anguish. He'd tried to warn Brad that insults from your childhood friends wouldn't feel the same as taunts from strangers.

Brad wasn't going to stay in Ames Bridge now. Why would he live in a place where people he'd once hung out with treated him like shit? Pax longed to splash cold water on his face, but he was sure he'd soak his shirt if he did, not that it mattered what he looked like at this point. He should just find Brad and get them out of there.

He should, but he didn't. He found himself needing to put off the inevitable. Brad would leave, maybe even the next day, and life would go back to the way it had been. He'd expected that, but now that the reality was here, he didn't want to face it.

After he exited the bathroom, he saw a group of teachers, some of whom he'd have liked to talk to, but Mrs. Sheffield and Mrs. Spindale were with them. The prayers they sent up for him to be cured of the demons of homosexuality were all the interaction he—or his immortal soul—needed to have with them.

His phone buzzed with a text from Brad. He knew he should answer, but he needed a few more minutes alone. He wandered the edge of the room, doing his best not to make eye contact with anyone. When he'd made it about halfway around, Brad called his name. Oh well, he'd put it off as long as he could.

"Why didn't you come find me?" Brad asked.

Great. Brad knew he'd been avoiding him. "I…uh…got caught up talking."

Brad's expression said he knew Pax was lying. "To whom?"

"Maybe we should go."

Brad sighed. He looked almost as hurt as he had when Luther tried to intimidate him.

"I just figured you wouldn't want to stay. Not after…"

"Luther being an ass? That's nothing. I just got snubbed by Mrs. Sheffield and overheard how gross it was that Wilson Knight used to shower with me."

"God, that sucks."

"It does." Brad drew in a breath and straightened his shoulders. "But I won't let them run me off."

No matter what he said, Pax could tell he'd lost the self-assurance he'd had before they arrived.

"Okay, but I—"

"You want to go."

"It's all too much, isn't it?"

Brad glanced around the room. "They did go a little overboard. It's tacky, even for a prom." He was trying so damn hard to lighten things up, but his smile was tight and strained.

"You know that's not what I mean."

"Then what exactly do you mean?" His voice had an angry edge Pax hadn't heard before. Maybe he should've gone along with Brad's deliberate misunderstanding.

"Nothing. I'll stay if that's what you want."

"What I want is…" Time seemed to stand still as Pax waited for him to say whatever it was. He didn't think he was going to like it.

The first bars of the slow-dance classic "Right Here Waiting for You" fell into the silence. It would have to be that song. Pax had been right here waiting for Brad for years. Except now he was too scared to fight for what he wanted, and Brad was too newly awakened to reality.

But the look of wariness on Brad's face faded. He gave Pax a slow once-over and tilted his head toward the dance floor.

Pax glanced toward the couples who were already there in each other's arms. Heterosexual couples. Could they do this? Should they?

"One slow dance and then we'll leave," Brad said.

Pax might as well take this chance, since he wasn't likely to get another one.

He tensed when Brad pulled him into his

arms, but after a few seconds, he gave in to the slow swaying and laid his head on Brad's shoulder. He deserved this. They deserved this. Their dancing wasn't hurting anyone.

As they turned together, he noticed Mandy and Rose at the edge of the dance floor and smiled. He and Brad were getting some dirty looks, but there were others who smiled at him when he caught their eyes. Then, as he grew more comfortable, he closed his eyes and let himself feel.

Out of the blue, a hand closed on his shoulder and yanked him back. He stumbled, but Brad held on to him, keeping him upright.

"What the hell do you think you're doing?" Brad growled.

Pax turned to see Troy behind him.

"I'm making sure you understand this kind of shit isn't welcome here."

"Leave them alone, Troy." This came from Scott, who ran up out of breath. Had he been chasing Troy?

"Hell no, I'm not going to leave 'em alone. Backing off is what's gotten this country to where people think this shit is acceptable."

"They're just dancing," Scott said.

The people near them stopped dancing and backed away. But they didn't go far. They clearly wanted to see the show.

"I'll give you three seconds to get the fuck out of here and then—"

Pax punched him.

Troy staggered back and fell on his ass. He sat there, staring up at Pax as blood ran from his nose.

Pax had never seen him look so stunned.

Scott took Troy's arm and pulled him up, but Troy shook him off when he got to his feet. He started to charge Pax, but Scott grabbed one arm, and Jack, who must have appeared when Pax wasn't looking, grabbed his other.

"Come on. We're getting out of here," Jack said in a tone Pax didn't think anyone would argue with.

As they dragged him off, Troy hollered about how he was going to sue Pax, but no one seemed to pay any attention to him. They were joined by Scott's wife and Troy's date, who looked disgusted. Hopefully, she wouldn't go home with him.

"Are you okay?" Brad asked when they were gone.

Pax had to think about it. He looked down at his hand, flexed it, and winced. "I think so."

"That's going to be sore."

Pax nodded.

Mandy appeared then with a makeshift ice pack. Pax just stood there looking at her, not sure what to say. Was he in shock?

Brad took the ice and pressed it against Pax's sore knuckles.

"Thanks," Pax finally said. Everything seemed far away and dim. He needed to get out of there.

***

Brad took Pax's arm, afraid he might pass out.

"Do you guys need a ride?" Mandy asked, looking at Brad.

"I'm fine," Pax said, but the words came out

oddly flat. Brad didn't like that at all. Pax hadn't looked at him other than a brief glance since he'd punched Troy.

"I don't think you ought to drive until you're feeling better," Mandy said.

"I've only had one drink since we got here," Brad said. "I'll drive him home."

"Are you sure?"

"I am. I wouldn't take a chance, not with him."

She smiled. "Okay."

Brad put his arm around Pax and steered him to the door. When they were part of the way to the car, Pax finally spoke.

"I can't believe I actually punched someone."

Brad smiled. "It was kind of hot. I've never had anyone defend me like that."

Pax made a sound between a snort and a sob. "I don't know what I was thinking."

"You were thinking you'd had enough."

"I guess so, and that you had too. I was tired of everyone proving me right."

Brad stopped walking. They were in the middle of the parking lot, but he didn't care. "Pax, I—"

Pax shook his head. "You don't have to say it. I warned you. I knew you didn't want to live here, but now you've seen why. It's okay. You can go back, and I…" His voice broke, and Brad felt a stab of pain deep in his chest. "I'll understand."

"Is that what you want?" Brad could barely get the words out. This wasn't a conversation to have in public, but it was like an emotional avalanche he no longer had the power to stop.

"What I *want*?"

For some reason, Pax's unwillingness to just give a straight answer filled him with rage. "Yes. Are you happy now?"

"What? No."

Pax's words barely registered with him. "Are you saying you aren't thrilled things went just like you said they would? Because they did. Now I feel like shit because most of the people who loved me in high school only see me as a fucking queer, not a cool athlete or a successful businessman or a guy who fell in love with his best friend's brother. Because they can't see—"

"Wait, what?"

Brad snorted. "As if you didn't know."

"Brad, I…"

"I love you, okay? But you're right; this won't work."

"Brad, that was never—"

"Yes, it was. You've been waiting for the ax to fall this entire time."

"No, I haven't. I…"

But Brad saw his eyes widen, and he knew the moment Pax realized Brad was right. "I guess prom night isn't going to go any better than it did senior year."

Pax shook his head. "I tried to warn you."

"If you'd tried to encourage me, that would've been a hell of a lot better."

He started walking again then, because if he didn't, he wasn't sure what he was going to do—crying was definitely an option, but anger and despair were warring it out for top billing.

He heard Pax's footsteps behind him. When they reached the car, Pax pulled out his keys. "I'm driving."

"No, you're not. You're shaken up from—"

"No more than you."

"Goddammit, Pax. You were so pale, and I—"

"I can drive."

He beeped the car open, and as Brad got into the passenger seat, he thought about the other evening he'd ridden with Pax, the one when he'd been stupid enough to do shots with Troy. He'd worried Pax wouldn't want anything else to do with him after he'd almost thrown up all over Pax's car. Now he felt sick again, but this time things weren't going to turn out as well as they did that night.

Why the fuck was Pax assuming he'd leave? Why was he determined this wasn't going to work?

Neither of them spoke during the drive to the motel. He could've told Pax that as much as the rejection had hurt, he had no plans to hightail it back to Chicago, but he'd gotten tired of trying to convince Pax that he loved him enough to face any consequences, and…if he were honest, he wasn't sure how he felt about moving to Ames Bridge. He had to admit he was disturbed by how vehement some people had been in their dislike of his "lifestyle." But he'd wanted to talk to Pax about it, to work it out between them. If only he were sure Pax was willing to do that.

"So you're just going to drop me off?" Brad wasn't sure why he phrased it as a question. Pax had all but said things were over.

"I don't think going in would be a good idea."

Brad nodded. "Right."

"I'm already going to miss you. Another night together would hurt too much."

"And that's what you want? For me to leave?"

"Isn't it what *you* want?"

"You haven't given me a chance to say what I want."

Pax looked away. "I… Yeah, I guess not, but in Chicago you can be open without getting shit from people who are supposed to be your friends. You can find someone who—"

"No! It's always been you, Pax. You've always been the one I wanted."

"But this all happened so fast, before you knew what it was really like to be out in Ames Bridge."

"It's been building since I was seventeen. Do you really think it's too fast, or is it too late?"

Pax sank his teeth into his lower lip and closed his eyes. "I don't know." His voice shook, and Brad couldn't take any more.

He opened his door and started to step out, but Pax grabbed his arm. "Wait. Please."

The anguish in his voice was all that kept Brad from shaking him off.

"What?" God, he sounded tired.

"What would you have said if… If I'd asked instead of assuming."

"That I'm scared, confused, surprised, but that you are more important than any of those assholes and I want to see if we can work something out."

Pax let out a long breath. "I'm sorry."

"For what exactly?"

"For...a lot of things, but mostly for not listening."

Brad nodded. "Thank you."

Pax smiled, just a brief lifting of one corner of his mouth, but it was enough to give Brad hope that the assholes at the prom hadn't ruined everything.

"I was protecting myself. I've learned to do that, to not seem too eager for anyone's acceptance, because then I won't be crushed when I don't get it."

"Oh, Pax. There are so many people in this town who love you."

"I know that, but..."

"You don't let them in. You don't let anyone in."

Pax looked away and drummed his fingers on the steering wheel. "You've only been here a few days. How can you know that?"

"Pax, I see you, the real you, even if you don't realize it."

"Don't leave tomorrow."

"Why?"

"Because I'd like to see you again, but I need some time to think."

Brad's chest tightened. He'd thought things were better, but... "Isn't that code for 'I'm breaking up with you'?"

Pax started to speak, but Brad interrupted him. "Because if it is, just say what you mean. If there's no hope for us, then I should leave."

"There's hope. That's not what I meant. And we can't break up since we're not—"

"Bullshit. If you tell me there's no chance for

us, that will be the biggest breakup of my life."

Pax's eyes widened, but he nodded. "Yeah. You're right." He reached out and cupped Brad's face. "Please don't leave town. I really do need some time, and I think you do too."

"I guess I do. Moving is a big step, and I tend to just jump in without a plan, but—"

"I like that about you," Pax said.

"You do?"

"Yeah."

Pax caressed his cheek with the pad of his thumb. Then he closed the distance between them and pressed his lips gently to Brad's.

Despite the tension, Pax's warm scent and the softness of his lips sent heat straight to Brad's cock. He wanted to bury his face in Pax's neck and breathe him in. Then he wanted to drag him inside and fuck him until he begged Brad to move to Ames Bridge. He pulled back before he lost his mind and tried to fulfill that fantasy.

"At least I know you want me, even if we're not going to act on it tonight."

Pax smiled. "I do. So very much."

"You still could come in." It would be so easy to channel his overabundance of emotion into lust.

But Pax shook his head. "Not tonight."

"The thought of not touching you again…"

"I know."

Brad pushed the door open, got out of the car, and walked away. But at the door, he turned back to watch Pax back out of his spot and drive off.

Chapter Eighteen

Pax's phone buzzed when he was almost back to his apartment. He pulled it out after he'd parked, expecting to see a text from Brad; instead, it was from his mom.

What was she doing up at... Oh, it was only ten. It hadn't taken all that long for the homophobes to send them on their way. He'd stayed later at his own prom despite hating that one too.

I hope you're having a good time. Your father and I wish you the best.

Was it normal for parents to text their children when they were out? Maybe his mom still thought he needed reassurance that they accepted him.

They didn't expect him to answer, did they? And yet, after all the unsettling events of the night—that was such a mild word for what it had been like—he wanted to talk to someone who'd fuss over him a little.

Brad would've fussed over you a lot if you'd let him.

He wasn't going to think about that.

He let himself into his apartment and called home.

"Paxton, is that you?" his mother said when she answered.

No, someone had stolen his cell in an Ames Bridge crime wave. "Yes, Mom."

"What are you doing calling us? You should be having fun with Brad."

"Well…um…"

"What's wrong, darling?"

"Things didn't go exactly like I'd hoped."

His mother sucked in her breath. "What happened? Are you okay?"

He hadn't meant to scare her. "Nothing you need to worry about. I'm fine."

"Do you need us to come over?"

He didn't like his parents driving late at night. "No, I'd have come there if I needed to."

"Where are you?"

"Home."

"So soon?"

"Some people objected to us being there." His mom would hear about it from someone—multiple someones—in the morning, so there wasn't any point hiding the details.

"Assholes."

"Mom!"

"Paxton you're thirty-four. I think I can say 'asshole' around you now."

"Right. Mrs. Sheffield wouldn't talk to Brad, but Troy Anderson and Luther Ledford said some awful things. Troy grabbed me when Brad and I were dancing, and I hit him."

His mother gasped. "You hit him?"

"Yes. Please don't be angry; he—"

"Angry? I'm not angry. I'm proud of you. You've taken too much nonsense from people like that."

Her support warmed him. He really was lucky

to have the parents he did. "Mom, I don't think I've thanked you enough for being there for me no matter what."

"Of course we're here for you. That's what family is for." If only all families believed that.

"Is Troy likely to take this further, son?"

Pax hadn't realized his father had gotten on the phone too. "I don't think so because he'd have to admit he got knocked down by a fag."

"Don't call yourself that," his mother scolded.

"I'm not. That's what he called me."

His father snorted. "I still can't believe Troy passed the bar. He should have his license revoked."

"For being an asshole?" Pax asked.

"Paxton," his father chided.

"Mom said it."

She laughed. "I did."

His father laughed too. "I suppose if they disbarred people for asinine behavior, we wouldn't have many lawyers left."

"That might be the case," Pax agreed.

"Are you okay?" his mom asked. "He didn't hit you back?"

"He tried to, but Scott Tregar and Jack—I can't remember his last name; he runs the inn—"

"Lawrence. Jack Lawrence."

"Right. They dragged Troy off."

"So Brad's there with you?" his mom asked.

"No, I dropped him off at his motel."

"Why?"

Heat rushed to his face. "Mom!"

"I just thought…"

"Brad and I aren't sure what we want. The

night shook both of us up. I tried to tell him it would be awful, and it was. I assumed he'd want to go back to Chicago—I guess you know he's been thinking about buying the Marsdon place?"

"I do," his mom said.

"And you didn't say a word about it while I was there? Even though that's where your corn came from?"

She sniffed. "I didn't think it was my place."

"Your place to—"

"Settle down, son," his father said. "We're trying to help."

Pax sighed. They didn't deserve to be snapped at. "I know. I'm sorry."

"Did you give Brad a chance to tell you what he wanted?" his mom asked.

Um...

"Pax?"

"Not really."

"Did you assume you knew what was best for him?"

"Like you're assuming that's what I'd do?" The peevish tone was back.

"Did you?"

"Yes." Damn, he hated how easily his mother could read him.

"No wonder he's pissed off at you."

"I didn't say he was—"

"He didn't come home with you."

"Maybe he—"

"Pax, I do understand how romance works."

He was not going to think about that.

"You should call him."

"We're going to talk again before he leaves, but we both agreed we needed time to think."

"Doesn't that mean you're breaking up?" she asked.

What was with everyone tonight? "We weren't even together."

"Paxton, I saw you together."

"No, I mean, we weren't in a relationship. We were just... I don't know."

"You've loved that man since you were in high school."

"I had a crush on him, but I..." *I love him. I've always loved him.*

"Yes, you do." That was from his dad. Pax was more clueless than *his dad.*

His heart pounded, and the world spun around him. He loved Brad. Somehow, despite how long it had been, he loved him. And not just the memories from high school, but the man he was now: smart, aggressive, encouraging. How could that not be worth it?

"I can't ask him to live in Ames Bridge."

"So don't," his mom said.

"But how—"

"You could both move to Greensboro." His dad wanted him to move?

"But the gallery is here."

"It's a thirty-minute commute. He probably goes farther than that in Chicago."

"Or you could let him decide what he wants to do," his mom said.

Why did they have all the answers? "You're right."

"I… Yes, I am."

He laughed. "Should I really call him now? If it's going to be his decision, shouldn't I give him time to think about it?"

"Not too much time. Text him or something. Let him know you care."

"Thanks, y'all. I love you."

"We love you too. Now go figure out what you're going to say to get your man back."

Pax groaned. "Mom, he's not my man, and I can't 'get him back' if we—"

"Pax, he's yours if you can find the courage to tell him how you feel."

He hated how right she was. "Okay. Good night."

"Good night," they both said.

As Pax ended the call, he thought about how Brad looked earlier with his face illuminated by the glow from a streetlamp, tired, discouraged, all because Pax was making assumptions instead of talking to him. Wasn't this what he'd wanted for years? Why was he pushing Brad away?

He brought up Brad's text screen. *I'm sorry I assumed you'd want to leave. I'll listen whenever you're ready.*

Brad still hadn't replied after Pax undressed and brushed his teeth. He still hadn't replied after Pax finished reading a few chapters in a thriller Cindy had recommended; or after he glanced through the headlines of the *Washington Post*.

Pax sighed. Was he really going to spend all night waiting for a text?

No, he was going to get some sleep. If Brad

hadn't texted him by morning, he would go over there and confess his stupidity in person.

He put his phone on Do Not Disturb, swallowed a few Tylenol PM, and then tossed and turned until they took effect.

***

After Pax left the night before, Brad had made use of the motel's gym, a.k.a a universal machine and a treadmill in a room that was basically a closet. Then he'd taken a long hot shower and gone to bed. He hadn't remembered he'd turned his ringer off at dinner and never turned it back on.

When he woke the next morning to bright sun streaming through his window, he reached for his phone to check the time and saw Pax's text.

Shit. Pax probably thought he was too pissed off to answer. But was he ready to talk to Pax? Did he know what he wanted?

He lay back and stared at the ceiling, studying the wiggly edges of a water stain. Last night had sucked. Well, not all of it. Dancing with Pax had been amazing. So had talking to Mandy, Rose, and Krishna and knowing that they and Jack, and even Scott, stood with him when it came down to it. Pax punching Troy was damn fine too. Knowing that skittish as Pax might be, he was ready to defend Brad, to defend their right to be a couple, gave Brad hope. Because the thought of kissing Pax goodbye for good and going back to Chicago made him ache all over.

He had a good life there, friends, work, sex if he wanted it. But what he wanted was Pax. Those soft sounds he made, the way he kissed Brad like he could do it all day, the way his hands tightened when he came… Having that was worth anything. The night before, in those moments when prejudice and disgust were battering him, he'd forgotten just how good loving and being loved felt. And he'd forgotten just how many friends they had in town: Cal and Beck, Trish, Elsie, Irene, and apparently also Jack.

He picked up his phone again, eager to let Pax know he was ready to talk, more than ready. He started composing his reply and then stopped.

He'd waited this long to text him. He could wait a little longer. Because instead of sending words that couldn't possibly express how he felt, he was going to show up at Pax's door and make clear to him once and for all that he was in love with him and had no intention of throwing that away.

Brad got dressed quickly and then went through the pockets of his suitcase, trying to remember where he'd put the CD he'd made for Pax before leaving Chicago. He'd felt ridiculous making a mix CD like they were still teenagers. It showed his age that he even still had a CD burner, but this week was supposed to be all about nostalgia, right? He'd brought it, but he hadn't been sure he'd have the nerve to actually give it to Pax. Now it was just what he—what *they*—needed.

He reached into the last of the interior pockets, and—yes! There it was, but wrapped in a plain white sleeve, it didn't look anything like a CD he would've gotten in high school.

Did he dare?

Oh, why the hell not. He found a pen—too bad he didn't have a pink one—drew hearts around the edges, and wrote a cheesy note. Pax might think he was crazy, but if he was going to make a final play for him, why not be over-the-top about it?

He needed more than a CD, though. What was something he knew Pax loved, something special that would let him know Brad paid attention when they talked? After a few seconds of thinking, he had it. Cookies. The iced ones Pax was obsessed with. He glanced at his phone. It was nine a.m. on a Sunday. The bakery wouldn't be open, but there was a good chance someone was already there, baking for the afternoon. Hopefully, it would be Paula. He'd dated her briefly in high school, and they'd remained friends. She didn't show up for the reunion prom, but he knew she'd taken over the bakery from her mother.

Heart pounding, he grabbed his wallet, keys, phone, and the CD and raced out the door.

Chapter Nineteen

A faraway pounding woke Pax. Was someone doing construction? On Sunday morning? He pulled the comforter over his head, which throbbed like he was hungover. That was unfair when he hadn't even had anything to drink. An emotional hangover? Damn, this was going to be a great day.

Before he could get back to sleep, his phone rang.

He pulled it under the covers with him and squinted at the bright screen. Shit! It was Brad.

"Um… Hello." Wow. Great start.

"I woke you up, didn't I?"

Was there a right or wrong answer to that? "Kinda. I was trying to get back to sleep."

"I'm here, and I'm ready to talk."

"Here as in at this building?"

"Yes."

Panic fluttered in his chest again. "I'm not dressed."

"That's fine by me."

His low, sexy voice had Pax's morning wood grow more insistent. "Okay, I'll be down in a minute."

"Don't rush."

"I… Okay."

He ended the call and slid out of bed. Fuck. What was he going to do? What was he going to say?

He'd been an idiot last night. He should've called Brad or gone back to his motel. What if now he...?

Go open the door.

Pax gave up on the idea of finding an outfit he looked good in. Instead he pulled on some ancient sweats with his *Lion King the Musical* T-shirt and took the stairs two at a time.

He yanked the door open like he was ripping off a Band-Aid. He needed this over and done. Needed to know...

Brad held out a bag. "This is for you."

"Oh."

"Oh?"

Pax shook his head. "I don't know what I was expecting, but— Wait, I smell icing."

Brad smiled. "You do."

Pax opened the bag and saw his favorite cookies, a lot of them. He could tell they'd just been made by how soft the icing looked. "The bakery doesn't open until one on Sundays. How did you...?"

"Paula was there. I bribed her."

"Wow. Thank you."

Brad pointed to the bag. "There's more in there."

Pax examined it again and discovered a CD against the side. He pulled it out and turned it over. Brad had decorated it with hearts and the words *Brad + Pax 4ever*.

Did he mean that seriously, or was it just nostalgia? Forever? Pax's heart pounded. He wanted that. He wanted forever with Brad.

"Can you..." He held out the bag to Brad, who took it so Pax could pull the CD out of its sleeve.

He needed to know what was on it and—yes, the songs were listed under the title, *Pax's Mix*, which Brad had written in bubble letters. The first song was "Open Your Heart."

Pax grabbed a fistful of Brad's T-shirt and yanked him inside the stairwell. Brad's mouth opened in surprise, and Pax used the opportunity to push his tongue in. The door slammed as he pushed Brad against it and then continued his efforts to devour him. After Brad got over the shock, he gave as much as he was getting, groaning as he explored every inch of Pax's mouth. By the time Pax pulled back to get some air, they were both hard as steel.

"Upstairs," Brad ordered.

Pax raced up the stairs as fast as he could, and Brad followed him. In his haste, he'd left the door to his apartment standing wide open.

Brad shut the door behind them. Pax took the bakery bag from him and set it and the CD down on a shelf. Then he pulled Brad to him again. He slid his lips from Brad's mouth, along his neck, nibbling and sucking and then pulling his T-shirt aside so he could sink his teeth into Brad's collarbone.

Brad growled and tightened his grip on Pax's hips. Then he lifted Pax so Pax straddled him, and pushed him up against the wall by the door.

"I love that you can do that," Pax said as he thrust against him, rubbing their cocks together.

"Lift you?"

"Uh-huh. It's fucking hot."

They worked their hips together. The friction was heavenly, and if he kept it up, he was going to come. He had no intention of stopping until he'd gotten both of them off.

Brad held on to his thighs, keeping Pax anchored against him, licking at his neck, nibbling, teasing, not giving him what he wanted. Brad chuckled against him, his breath tickling Pax's skin. "You're ferocious."

"I know what I want now," Pax said breathlessly.

"And that is?"

"You. All of you and not just today."

"Mmm. Good, because you're mine."

Brad's possessive declaration made Pax shiver, and he protested when Brad stepped back, forcing him to lower his legs. He swayed when he got his feet on the ground, but Brad steadied him.

"Don't want to stop," Pax protested.

"I have no intention of stopping for long, but I want you in a bed where I can take my time with you."

"No."

Brad raised a brow. "You really want to fuck against the wall?"

"Mmm. Maybe, but wherever we are, I don't want slow."

Brad laughed. "I want to work you over until you're panting, begging, ready to die if I don't fuck you."

Just hearing Brad talk like that might push him over the edge. "Yes, but do that fast."

Pax started to pull off his T-shirt, but Brad grabbed his hands. "Slow down."

"Why? You said—"

"Don't you think we should talk first?"

Pax had promised Brad he'd listen, but after the cookies and the CD, he'd lost his mind. His heart pounded.

Say it.

"Brad, I've wanted you forever, and seeing that CD made me realize I'm more afraid of losing you than anything else. It's been a long time since I've given myself permission to have what *I* want, but I want you and...if you..."

"I love you, Pax."

"I love you too, so much."

Brad pulled Pax into his arms, and Pax let himself sink into Brad's strength as they held each other tight. Then he nuzzled Brad's neck, breathing in his scent. He could stay like this forever. Brad shifted, and their cocks rubbed together.

"That's how I knew I was gay," Pax said.

"Because you like sniffing me?"

He pulled away, heat rising in his face. "No."

"But you do."

He nodded. "Yeah, you smell great, but do you remember the day when Julie Hartwell made my brother a mix tape?"

"You sat on the couch, trying to pretend you weren't listening to everything Rob and I said."

Pax nodded. "She put 'Open Your Heart' on the CD."

"And I wanted to listen to it."

"You sang along with it, and as I watched you, I realized you were a lot more to me than my brother's cool friend."

Brad's smiled widened. "You looked at me that day—and most days after—like I'd hung the moon."

Had he really been that bad? "Did you know?"

"That you had a crush on me?"

"Yeah."

"I'm not sure I could have put it into those words. I knew you really liked me, and I think maybe I had a sense of what that meant, but I wasn't ready to accept that I felt the same way about you, so I ignored it until months later when we were wrestling."

"Why the hell did it take us this long to realize we love each other?"

"I don't know, but at least we finally did."

"So what do we do?"

"I buy the Marsdon house and…we move in?"

"But last night you said—"

"I was hurt and confused, and you—"

"I was awful."

"Not so awful. You did punch Troy to defend me."

Pax winced. "Yeah, I did, but then I told you how to feel instead of listening to you."

"But it didn't stop me from loving you. I still want to be right here with you."

"We could move to Greensboro. I could commute from there."

Brad shook his head. "I want to try this. I want us to be where we can help your parents and you can go back and forth to the gallery without it being a long trip. If we hate it, I'll rent the house or sell it, and we'll move."

"You make it sound easy."

Brad cupped his face. "I don't think it's going to be easy; not at all. And I will have to travel often.

But if we're together, I believe we can make it work."

Pax smiled. "Me too. Can we get naked now?"

Brad laughed as he tugged on Pax's shirt, encouraging him to lift his arms.

After tossing the shirt to the ground, he kissed Pax and ran his hands along Pax's bare back. He started backing them toward the bedroom as they kissed. Eventually, they hit the edge of the mattress and tumbled, Brad falling on top of him. He opened his legs so Brad could fit between them, and after several delicious moments of kissing and grinding on each other, Brad sat back and pulled his shirt over his head.

Pax licked his lips as he studied Brad's bare chest. "Keep going."

He undid his pants and rose up on his knees to start working them down. Pax whistled when his cock sprang free. Then he worked as quickly as he could to get his own pants off. When they were both completely naked, Pax reached for him. "I want to taste you."

Brad moved up his body until he could brush his cock over Pax's lips. Pax ran his tongue along the underside and cupped Brad's heavy balls, rolling them in his hand. Then he opened up and took Brad in, slipping a few fingers into his mouth alongside Brad's shaft, getting them good and wet with spit.

When he pushed a finger into Brad's ass, Brad groaned, pushing back against the digit. Then he thrust forward, driving farther into Pax's mouth. Pax added a second finger, and Brad worked himself between Pax's stimulation of his ass and the heat of Pax's mouth. He moved faster and faster, and Pax sucked harder, tugging on his balls with his other hand.

"Stop!" Brad shouted, and reluctantly Pax pulled his fingers from Brad's ass and let his cock slip from his mouth. Brad shifted position until he was stretched out beside Pax.

What the hell was he doing? "Aren't you going to...?"

"Fuck you now?" Brad asked.

He nodded frantically.

"I want to explore some first. I want slow, remember?"

Pax scowled. "Fuck slow."

"Yeah, we could do that too."

"The hell we will."

Brad laughed, the sound rich and intoxicating, and Pax feared he would go crazy before he got Brad where he wanted him, fucking Pax so deep, he was full all the way to his throat.

Brad touched his cheek. "I love you."

Pax smiled, everything but those words momentarily forgotten. "I love you too."

Brad pushed at his shoulder, encouraging him to roll to his stomach. Then he kissed, licked, and nibbled his way down Pax's back. When he reached the top of his ass, he bit down, making Pax gasp.

"Like that?"

"Fuck, yes!" He thrust against the mattress, trying to get relief.

When Brad ran his tongue over the tops of his ass cheeks, Pax pushed back, silently begging for what he wanted. Brad made a sound like a purr as he nuzzled into Pax's crack, then grabbed his cheeks and pulled them apart. "Yes, please," Pax begged, coming up on his knees.

Brad kept teasing, licking his tailbone, biting into the fleshy part of his ass, all while holding him open, exposed. Then, finally, he tongued Pax's hole, making him see stars. The sensation of Brad licking and then pushing in was the most intense feeling he'd ever experienced.

Brad gave him no mercy, spearing him with his tongue, pushing in as far as he could, then adding fingers too. It felt so damn good. Pax had to reach between his legs and squeeze the base of his cock to hold himself back. He cursed and muttered nonsense as Brad kept going, pushing him almost to tears with longing.

Then he sat back, smacked Pax's ass, and said, "Turn over," in that commanding tone that was enough to make Pax desperate for him without the life-changing rimming he'd just received.

Pax flopped onto his back and stroked himself as he stared at Brad, forgetting that he wanted to hold off.

Brad seized his wrist and tugged. "Hands over your head."

Pax whimpered, not wanting to stop, but Brad glared at him. "You've waited this long, you can wait a little more."

Pax shook his head.

"Not long now, I promise." Brad stroked his thighs, making him squirm.

"I've been wanting you since I was fourteen," Pax complained. "We've got a lot of time to make up for."

Brad laughed. "Lube? Condom?"

"In the drawer." Pax tilted his head toward the nightstand as he reached up, latching onto his pillow like it was a life preserver.

He watched as Brad covered his cock and slicked it up.

"You do know I want this as badly as you do, right?" Brad asked, and Pax realized Brad's hands were shaking.

"I love you," he said, wanting to reassure him, but also simply enjoying being able to say it.

"Good." Brad pushed Pax's legs up onto his chest, guided his cock to his entrance, and held his gaze as he pushed forward; Pax lay not moving, not even breathing.

Brad didn't hold back, and Pax's ass burned as his thick cock worked all the way in. *Too much*, his mind screamed.

"Relax." Brad wrapped a hand around Pax's cock and stroked.

"I can't. I'm feeling so much—us loving each other, you staying here, you splitting me in two."

Brad supported himself on one hand and stroked Pax's face. "You're thinking about too much at once. Just open yourself to me and feel."

Open your heart.

That's what he had to do, because this was so much more than just amazing sex.

"I'm scared," he confessed.

Brad nodded. "Me too."

Just hearing him say it, watching the concern on his face, knowing that he didn't care what a mess Pax was, allowed him to release his tension. He moaned as Brad pulled out and slowly filled him again. He kept going, in and out, making Pax's body light up with pleasure.

Pax started to move too. Brad's thrusts came faster until Pax was bucking up, fighting him while telling him he goddamn better fuck him into the mattress. Pleasure built, pushing Pax higher and higher, and then he let go, his emotions spilling out along with the pent-up desire he'd hidden for years. In that moment, he knew without a doubt that they were going to make this work.

Brad's orgasm followed soon after, and he drove into Pax, clutching his hips so tight, Pax was sure he'd have bruises, but he didn't mind at all.

"Why did we wait so long?" Brad's words whooshed out of him as he sank heavily onto Pax, making him sputter. Pax wiggled, trying to push him off.

Laughing, Brad rolled to his side, and they lay there, trying to catch their breaths. When he was capable of speech, Pax said, "Do you think we can make up for all the time we've lost?"

"I have every intention of trying, because that was fucking amazing."

Pax nodded even though Brad wasn't looking at him. "Give me a minute, and we'll get started on the next round."

"I'm older, remember? I may need a little more time and some breakfast."

Pax looked him up and down and said, "You look healthy enough to me, but I guess I can spare a cookie."

Brad laughed as Pax dragged himself to the

living room to retrieve the bakery bag. "If only mix tapes had worked that well back in high school."

"Julie would've had Rob wrapped up like a package," Pax said.

Brad looked suddenly serious. "I miss him."

"Me too." Pax set the bag down and pulled Brad into his arms. "I guess we'll always miss him. I just hope…"

"Yeah?"

"I hope if he knows about us, he's okay with it."

Brad kissed the top of his head. "I think he is."

They lay like that, holding each other so long that Pax was in danger of falling asleep. He disentangled himself and sat up. "Want a cookie?"

"Yes!" Brad said.

"Are you serious about me moving in with you?" Pax asked when they'd each taken a few bites.

"Do we get to do this every night?"

"Hell yes!"

"Then I'm all for it." Brad took his hand, then rubbed his thumb over Pax's palm. "Seriously, I want you there."

"I want to be there. But it will be strange to be in a real house, right there next door to Elsie, in the midst of Ames Bridge society."

Brad snorted. "I can't argue with that."

"I've gotten used to having a little privacy here."

"Hopefully the neighbors will learn to leave us alone, or they'll get an eyeful."

Pax grimaced. "I'd like to think we'd scare them away, but some of them are way too curious."

Brad held up a hand. "Don't say that."

He ate the rest of his cookie and looked around. "I can't say I'll mind us having more space."

Pax laughed. "A larger bed would be nice."

"And a larger shower."

"But until then, um, do you want to stay here? I know it will be cramped, but…"

"Wherever you are, that's where I want to be."

"Me too."

Brad smiled. "I like this new attitude of letting yourself have what you want."

"You do?"

"Yes. So what else do you want to do?"

Pax considered the question for a few moments. There were so many things he'd put off. Finally, he had an answer. "Horse-riding lessons. I talked to Cal about them, but I never set them up."

Brad tilted his head like he was considering that. "I've done bungee jumping, parachuted from a plane, and cliff-dived in Acapulco, but I've never ridden a horse."

"Wow. I… I've ridden a horse, but only a gentle one on a trail ride. You don't expect me to…"

"No, we'll find adventures to share, but they don't have to be that daring. We could take riding lessons together and then explore the trails."

Pax narrowed his eyes. "Is this just a scheme to have me in the woods after all?"

He held Pax's gaze and licked his lips. "Maybe." He palmed his cock, stroking slowly. "I was just thinking."

Pax thought he might like this line of thinking. "What?"

"I could give you a riding lesson right now."

"Oh, could you now?"

"Hell yes."

Pax reached into the drawer for another condom. "Show me what you've got for me, cowboy."

Brad pulled Pax on top of him, and after Pax had readied him, he lowered himself onto Brad's cock, gasping at how well Brad filled him up. He started off slow, then worked up to an easy trot, then a canter, and finally a full-on gallop. They gasped, cursed, and clawed at one another, and when Pax's climax crashed over him, he shouted Brad's name, knowing Brad was his and that was how things were meant to be. The locks on both their hearts were open, and they fit together perfectly.

Dear Reader,

Thank you for purchasing *The Past Comes Home*. I hope you enjoyed it. *Down on the Farm*: *Ames Bridge* Book 1 is available now, and Book 3 is coming in December 2017. If you'd like to read another book set in North Carolina, check out *Coming Clean*. If you like gay erotic romance you may also enjoy the *Thorne and Dash* series which starts with *Professional Distance.* I offer a free book to anyone who joins my mailing list. To learn more, go to silviaviolet.com/newsletter.

Please consider leaving a review where you purchased this ebook or on Goodreads. Reviews and word-of-mouth recommendations are vital to independent authors.

I love hearing from readers. You can email me at silviaviolet@gmail.com. To read excerpts from all of my titles, visit my website: silviaviolet.com.

Silvia Violet

Author Bio

Silvia Violet writes erotic romance in a variety of genres including paranormal, contemporary, and historical. She can be found haunting coffee shops looking for the darkest, strongest cup of coffee she can find. Once equipped with the needed fuel, she can happily sit for hours pounding away at her laptop. Silvia typically leaves home disguised as a suburban stay-at-home-mom, and other coffee shop patrons tend to ask her hilarious questions like "Do you write children's books?" She loves watching the looks on their faces when they learn what she's actually up to. When not writing, Silvia enjoys baking sinfully delicious treats, exploring new styles of cooking, and reading to her incorrigible offspring.

Website: silviaviolet.com

Facebook: facebook.com/silvia.violet

Twitter: @Silvia_Violet

Pinterest: pinterest.com/silviaviolet

Instagram: silvia.violet

Titles by Silvia Violet

Revolutionary Temptation
Coming Clean
If Wishes Were Horses
Needing A Little Christmas
Astronomical
Meteor Strike

Fitting In
Fitting In
Sorting Out
Burning Up
Going Deep

Thorne and Dash
Professional Distance
Personal Entanglement
Perfect Alignment
Well-Tailored (A Thorne and Dash Companion Story)

Ames Bridge
Down on the Farm
The Past Comes Home
Tied to Home (Coming December 2017)

Unexpected
Unexpected Rescue
Unexpected Trust
Unexpected Engagement

Law and Supernatural Order
Sex on the Hoof
Paws on Me
Dinner at Foxy's
Hoofing' It To The Altar

Wild R Farm
Finding Release
Arresting Love
Embracing Need
Taming Tristan
Willing Hands
Shifting Hearts
Wild R Christmas

Available from Dreamspinner Press
Denying Yourself
Pressure Points

Made in the USA
Middletown, DE
17 July 2018